I0651550

Robert W. Bigham

California Gold-Field Scenes

Selections from Quien Sabe's Gold-Field Manuscripts

Robert W. Bigham

California Gold-Field Scenes
Selections from Quien Sabe's Gold-Field Manuscripts

ISBN/EAN: 9783337275280

Printed in Europe, USA, Canada, Australia, Japan

Cover: Foto ©Andreas Hilbeck / pixelio.de

More available books at **www.hansebooks.com**

California
Gold-field Scenes:

Selections from

Quien Sabe's Gold-field Manuscripts.

BY REV. R. W. BIGHAM,

Of the North Georgia Conference. Author of "Vinny Leal's Trip to the Golden Shore."

Introduction by A. G. Haygood, D.D., LL.D.

Nashville:
Southern Methodist Publishing House.
1886.

EDITOR'S NOTE.

THE "California Gold-field Scenes" will give many pleasant hours to the traveler by land or sea. The Author's style is peculiar, but it was inspired by his surroundings in the strange and marvelous country that has opened many new chapters in the history of the world. There are no dull descriptions, no tedious notes of travel, no wearisome reflections. Every thought is fresh and bright and new, and as striking as the scenery depicted in the volume. Young readers will be amused and instructed, and those of more matured experience will recognize the thrilling power of the Author's pen.

W. P. HARRISON,

Nashville, April, 1886. *Book Editor.*

Entered, according to Act of Congress, in the year 1886,
BY THE BOOK AGENTS OF THE METHODIST EPISCOPAL CHURCH, SOUTH,
in the Office of the Librarian of Congress, at Washington.

(2)

CONTENTS.

(3)

INTRODUCTION.

—

IT was years ago the good fortune of the writer of this introductory note to bring to the acquaintance of the young people of the firesides and Sunday-schools in the South a little book that made more friends than almost any other that has been issued by the Southern press. "Vinny Leal" and her "Trip to the Golden Shore" has held the fascinated attention of many thousands. As the booksellers say, "Vinny" had "a great run," many thousand copies having been printed and sold. It found a place in most of our Sunday-school libraries, and was read and read till worn out. And no wonder; for, while its author bound himself by none of the conventional rules of book-making, he somehow "had a knack" of making people see what he had seen, hear what he had heard, know and love the people he had known and loved. The writer of this Introduction saw in the Publishing House at Nashville what he never saw elsewhere—a printer break into tears while "setting up copy" for "Vinny Leal;" and he confesses to a similar

(5)

experience while "reading proof" as the book was "passing through the press."

The scenes, incidents, narratives, and characters that make up the body and soul of the "California Gold-field Scenes" will—if people's tastes and dispositions have not changed very much during the last fifteen years—make for this little book among the young people of to-day fully as many friends as learned to love "Vinny Leal;" while many who laughed and wept with the saintly maiden long ago will for their own sakes read what "Quien Sabe" has to tell them of the wonder-land on the Pacific. And not a few of these children of 1873 who took delight in "Vinny Leal" will now find a sweeter pleasure in reading the "California Gold-field Scenes" to their children of 1886.

The regulation critics will hardly approve the style and manner of our author. One would be glad to please them, if it did not cost too much; yet their approval is not necessary to the success or usefulness of a book. The conventional publisher's manuscript "taster" does not always know a book when he samples it. The history of books "declined with thanks" by prudent publishers would itself make a large and entertaining —perhaps instructive—volume. We may be sure that Bunyan's "Pilgrim" was not approved when first he sought acquaintance with publishers. It is almost incredible, but the informed on such subjects tell us that "Robinson Crusoe" was declined by publisher after publisher and returned to its author. After a long waiting a plucky publisher, who had little to lose by his venture, braved the critics and gave "Robinson Crusoe" to type and leather. Thackeray failed to find a publisher of "Vanity Fair," and was obliged to bring it out as a magazine serial story. It is said of the most charming of story-tellers of our times—Hans Christian Andersen—that his first venture was declined by every publisher in Copenhagen.

It is vain to criticise the structure of "Quien Sabe's" sentences, or the peculiarities of his idiom; it is as irrelevant to measure his "style" by the classics of English composition as to test the merits of a poem written in a newly invented meter by the verse of Virgil or Pope. Enough for his purpose he has of style; he makes us camp with him, dig gold with him, see the cascades and the sunsets, and hear the many voices of the day and night in the California gold-fields, as he saw and heard them.

So many evil things creep into young people's books nowadays that careful fathers and mothers must watch to see what manner they are of, just as they watch new play-fellows and acquaintances. But they need not be afraid of " Quien Sabe " and his friends—not the roughest and most uncouth of them. The spirit of the book is good; it will suggest pure thoughts and inspire noble sentiments; the gospel is in it all, because pure thoughts, noble sentiments, and the living gospel are in the author of the book, the Rev. Robert W. Bigham, an honored member of the North Georgia Conference, and one of the first missionaries to the gold coast in the early days of California.

ATTICUS G. HAYGOOD.

OXFORD, GA.

CALIFORNIA GOLD-FIELD SCENES

--◁-✳-▷--

CHAPTER I.

A WAIL SHRILLER THAN THE STORM'S.

IFE has its phantoms that tangle it in brambles. Yet the wounds of the brambles sometimes impart to life a grace and a joy that painlessness and ease can never bestow. So we will not dispel the gold-phantom because it enchants and draws us through jungles before admitting us within the gates to see the castles vanish and to collect the few real pearls their delusive structures contained. No phantom charmed like it. Its stretches of thorn are painted in hues of beauty and filled with songs to cheer us as we journey through them; and we almost forget the cares of the way for the caresses of the pure, glad scenes and sounds it places among the brambles. It pictured life and riches on the California gold-fields so deftly and thrillingly that infatuated multitudes gathered there from all climes

(9)

to revel in the witchery of gold. I went ashore among them one bright morning in 1850 on the sands of San Francisco.

The phantom's halo was upon every thing. The white-winged gulls, the gleaming atmosphere, the bluffy columns of the Golden Gate, the laughing bay, the dreaming isles, the misty brows of the Coast Range, the wrinkled prongs of Mt. Diablo, the excited faces of the surging passengers—ship, sea, land, sky—seemed tinged with gold. Albeit, the tinge was all; itself, the gold, was far away—snuggled, rock-locked, under the Sierra snow-crags.

Thither, exchanging the scalpel for the implements of the mineralist, I hurried on with the tumultuous throng, and pitched camp beneath a jetting ledge of coarse marble. My partner had been chosen with exceeding care, I thought—Tom Rothleit, an impulsive lawyer, whose forefathers, I learned from himself, had been distinguished for industry. The blood certainly had eliminated that quality before he felt its flow in his veins; yet he conceited that he and diligence would some day leave the world together, so closely were they allied. He was fond of *resting*, and I often queried, as the fitful months grated by, how he had redeemed time from that loved employ to learn to read and converse in several foreign languages, and to store his mind with the lore of many philosophies. His heart too was gentle as a mother's, and David's was no braver when he leaped to the fray with the gigantic hero of Gath.

The abyssmal placer we mined recoiled from the sky down deep among the roots of the beetled heights, and moaned in the throes of tempest and avalanche. A river clear as a diamond laughed at its grum features, and splashed them with icicles as it frolicked through the storm, and hissed us with defiant jeers as it swirled down its crabbed channel toward the far-away sea. We had toiled for a month, and only rare pebbles were the gems we had found. But Tom was persistent—perhaps I should say sullen—and we widened the pit, seeking the golden lead.

The day was the drearest. The thunderless storm shrieked along the gorges, or, falling down the mountains amid floods of sleet, froze upon bluff and chasm. I was prying a chiespa from a crevice in the bed-rock when a wail shriller than the storm's and the crash of the mine's steep bank told me that Tom was buried alive. I had repeatedly warned him to quit gouging about under there with his Bowie-knife, and to help scale up the bed-rock with a pick; but he said the point of the pick would slip on the ice and trip him, and he could almost see a big nugget, he thought. So he kept on in *his* industrious way, and now the catastrophe had him. Not a motion of the débris upon him guided to the spot where he lay. But as I rolled aside bowlder after bowlder in frenzied haste, a stranger leaped into the pit; and plunging here and there in the deepening slush we soon found him, and tenderly bore him to the camp; for we thought he was dead. It was only a few minutes after we had deposited his burly form near the fire when he revived; and so nonchalant was his leisurely yawn, as he sat up and glanced at the visitor inquiringly, that but for the huge bumps upon his forehead and scalp we might have thought that he had lain so still under the pebbled débris only to dupe us into the labor of lifting him out and bearing him to the camp. He was several days in regaining his appetite, however; and by that token, as much as by any other, I knew that he had suffered intensely; for the pleasures of eating moderately were known to him only when sick or through what he had read of and admired in the habits of others. He had too a way of giving no signs of his pains, lest they should inflict care upon others, though any pain in another met in him the nicest sympathy. Every thing we did, however awkwardly, pleased him. So we nursed him anxiously till he could straighten himself up and walk about the ledgy placer safely; and in a few weeks he was as well as ever.

Our visitor grew restless when Tom had passed the crisis of his hurt. He was quite young, of slender build, thin, pale, save now and then a flush clung first to one cheek then to the other; and he declined to share the mine with us on the plea of inadequate health. Leaving his name—Hal S.—with us, he departed whither we knew not, nor did he appear to care.

CHAPTER II.
HIS JEWELED FINGERS PRESSED THE HARP.

VEN at that early period, Cali-
fornia was infested by gambling-
hells in the cities of the valleys
and in the towns that grew as
if by magic along the gloomy
cañons by which the mountains were cleft in
twain. Though sinks of infamy, they were
usually attractive. Their lights were brilliant,
great log-fires blazed upon the hearths, choice
lunches lured on convenient tables, newspapers from many States were free to all, music
waltzed through their aisles; while piles of
gold and the courtesies of the proprietors allured to their deadly circles men of every
grade to be wrecked forever. One of them,
like an outpost of Satanism, sentineled the
trading-post whither Tom delightedly journeyed on occasion after supplies—his special-
ty was gastronomy. I know not what—his
"socialness," he said—led him within its
doors, whence he managed to escape alive, but
just alive, and how he could never tell.

Though often a bedlam, such a place was now and then stilled as each votary of its mocking goddess was awed by Vesper, and no sounds were heard save the soft fall of the cards and the subdued click of the dice. It was in the silence of such an interval, while Tom sat beholding the various groups in breathless contest for the piles of gold between them, that the notes of a harp floated upon the scene. They seemed to ravish simultaneously every ear, to touch to gentleness each heart; and after a short prelude the sounds, like music in ecstasy, were mingled with a young voice—low, brave, sad—that entranced dealer and diceman in mid-throw, and drew all eyes to the girlish-looking youth of nineteen summers as his jeweled fingers pressed from the harp its utmost melody. He looked as though he was conscious of having stepped from an Eden into a scene where no fruit pleasant to the eye or to the taste survived, and was throwing back across the separating gulf he had just passed to the loved ones he had left the last holy notes of a lost heart weeping over its ruined life. As the last chord of the song, "The Old Folks at Home," was struck he leaned the instrument against the rough column where he had found it, and stood some moments contemptu-

ously observing the scene. Many a storied
tear had shaded the eyes of the hardened sons
of chance as the old song's sentiment, like the
angel of Bethesda, troubled their hearts; and
they seemed for a moment to be dazed by the
visions of childhood the song had recalled, and a
few of them went out of " the hell " to return no
more. But directly the banker's quiet invita-
tions to the games were answered by the gold-
en nuggets upon the hazard again. And as
Hal, forgetful of his song, pushed into the
thick of the sporting groups and placed a
golden eagle upon a card, old Judge T., who
had intently watched him, said: "So he *falls*
—falls this time forever. He is a bold, kind,
cultured lad from a polished Western home,
and but lately vowed by his dead mother's
name to gamble no more. What a vice! Father living, mother sainted, not any friend
nor dearest memory can break the spell upon
him now. It is out of a heaven into h—l the
princely boy has plunged."

But ere the Judge's monologue had died
upon the clinky din of the saloon, Hal's purse
had doubled by the turn of a card, and he sat
watching his alternately increasing and diminishing pile of gold as though only it were
worth a thought beneath the studded sky.

While so absorbed a self-poised miner entered
the saloon and coolly scanned the many tables
till his eye, resting on Hal, blazed as if it
would sink the place to the perdition that
names it. Moving to the youth's side and
bending over him, he quietly said: "Come,
Hal; let's go now. We have far to walk
through the jungle, and the night wears away.
Let's start."

Without lifting his eyes, he replied: "You
here! Thought you would not venture out to-
night. Indisposed, you said." But, pondering
a moment, he added: "Wait till I play one
more game, then I'll go."

The miner looked ruefully upon him, but
lounged away to a reading group where Tom,
as it happened, was remarking the incident.
When the game ended he returned to Hal, and
pleasantly said: "It was well played; but
come, the moon is hiding behind the mountain; let's go tentward."

Hal half rose from his seat, but quickly sat
down again as the tables of gold swam before
his eyes. His face hardened till each feature
appeared like chiseled marble. Prouha's fa-
mous statue, "La Verité Vengeance," exhibits
no more implacable purpose than that which
chilled him to his place next the glistening

2

piles of gold. The phantom's wand was upon him. Its voice of golden melody had whispered him into an ecstasy of hope and purpose to own the glowy heaps that, like the treasures of enchantment, unfolded their riches to his witched gaze. His soul now had neither vision nor ear nor thought for any thing but gold.

Laying his hand lightly upon his arm, his friend added: "You promised, and I waited; come!"

Drinking deeply of a goblet of brandy by him, he replied in a bitter tone: "I will not go. You vex me; you do so incessantly. Why be so concerned about me?"

"No wrath, Hal; no wrath," he answered. "I may need your aid winding among the dark cliffs; and of late robbers infest the trails, you know. I shall feel greater security with company."

"Ah!" he retorted; "you afraid of Mexican outlaws, and among the first to scale Chapultepec a few years ago, held by their picked troops? And I never heard before that you were wont to totter from crags. The grizzly is not surer of foot among his natal chasms. No; that's a ruse. You have foiled my gaming as often as you shall. Go."

"You are right!" exclaimed several voices in the group. "Besides, you have won heavily of us, and must give us a chance to recover our losses."

"But," said the miner to him, not noticing them, "the choice to retire is yours. You can return whenever you will."

The gamblers now fiercely interposed, clicking their revolvers in the miner's face, and Hal, whose anger fired as they threatened his friend, felled the bruskest with a huge nugget; and Tom leaping to his help, the fierce fray of blows, shots, and stabs ceased only when the lights were quickly extinguished as the promptest means to quell the frantic mêlée.

CHAPTER III.

IF LEINA WERE HERE.

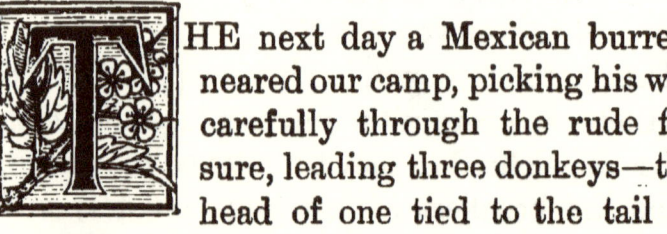HE next day a Mexican burrero neared our camp, picking his way carefully through the rude fissure, leading three donkeys—the head of one tied to the tail of the other, each burdened with a helpless man.

After the Mexican and I had laid the two guests upon all the blankets in the camp, Tom said, as we were taking him off his donkey: "I know you think me a greater ass than the one I ride; but I could not help it." And glancing to the wounded guests, he added: "They massed against them in the gambling-hell, and I tried to rescue."

"You mean that you rescued!" exclaimed Hal as he sprung to his elbow, but fell as suddenly prone again from utter exhaustion.

We placed Tom upon an old rubber coat or two, and as we wiped the gush of blood from his mouth a faint smile sickened on his cheek, and he whispered: "It's nothing, Quien; I'll be ready for the mine to-morrow."

Albeit, he lay like the dead for many hours after that. But his words, "I tried to rescue" and "It's nothing," were the key-notes to his character—bodied a spirit that never faltered to peril for the weak or to cheer others, whatever the torture that wrung himself. He had recognized Hal S. the moment the harp's notes had turned his eyes upon him in the saloon as the person who had helped to extricate him from death when the mine "caved in" upon him.

The magic of the gold-field, two years before this incident, had hazed Hal in an Atlantic college and wafted him to California, where the vice of cards promptly spunged from his heart the high purposes that adorn the average college-boy. Dissipation was rapidly mining out his life, for already consumption had paled and splotched his cheeks when the fatal wounds befell him in the gambling rencounter.

One night as we nursed him he grew colder and clammier, and weak to extremity, despite every care; and he whispered to us eagerly in a rhapsodic way: "You can't—help—me out —of—this. It is death. Van often warned me—of—it; warned—me that—sin and—life —are too unlike to abide long together, in me

—at—least; and there is no—help—for me—
now."

The sounds that phrased the last several
words were like one imagines the tones of the
soul would be if it were bruised into sobs.
And he lay very still, looking from face to
face as if to catch a gleam of hope from one
or another. But he closed his eyes as though
our despairful looks made gloomier his drear
wretchedness. Presently he said: "The shadow on the silent river darkens—now, and—in
its—awful hush—of—life—no sweet—note
comes—to—cheer—me in the—thickening
dark." And his eyes widened as he sighed
out the words, and were dimmed too as if life
were just then gone; but it was not, for he
murmured, with long pauses between the words:
"Innocence is peace; but crime—it makes life
a tangle-wild of thorns, and infuses death with
the bitterness of hopeless remorse."

His cold lips scarcely moved, yet his words
echoed in the ear definitely, though whispered
softly almost as a flutter of the death-angel.
He said: "How fatal the arrows *that* bowman
sin doth shoot! They wound to death quickly
body and soul. Soul! What is soul? Thought's
fountain, passion's electric sky, the likeness of
God. The angels shivered at sight of the an-

guish the pure Christ suffered to save it. But I, frenzied with gambling and brandy, have deemed *it* a trifle; mocked its upward longings; maddened it with a life of guilt till, on eager wing, it is flitting away forever—I know not whither."

Then he lay so motionless we thought he was dead. We could not see nor hear him breathe. But only the angel of sleep had touched him; yet we were conscious that a soul was disentangling itself from the ruins of its earthhome. The moon had dipped below the horizon, the skies had pulled thick vapors between them and the scene, and from the darkness of the chasm gusts of wind leaped about us as we kept vigil by the dying youth. The day broke and shed upon the crags its pale light, and brighter grew coming dawn to us, tinting and waking up all nature, and floated into the tent and fell about the dying one. It seemed —the voice of the light, was it?—to say something to his soul that startled and amazed it: For his eyes opened wide and wandered solemnly, intently from space to space, while tears and smiles joyfully commingled. Tom bent toward him, and asked, "What is it, Hal?"

"My mother, Tom," he answered; "my melody-voiced mother, who died a year ago. She

was here a moment ago. I felt her hand upon
my brow as it was wont to rest there, Tom,
when I was a child. And her loving lips sung
her favorite hymn—

> Just as I am, without one plea,
> But that Christ's blood was shed for me.

Ha! here again? Mother! Hist! she sings."

And wistfully, attently listening, as if catching with the heart syllabled mercy, each death-
line on his cold face lit with joy, he whispered:

> 'Just as I am, and waiting not
> To rid my soul of one dark blot.
> To thee whose blood can cleanse each spot,
> O Lamb of God, I come, I come!'

Precious blood shed for—me! . Saved, saved
by my mother's Christ. Praise!"

And his face was a vision of rapture as he
turned, gasped, and was dead. Our reverential posture was not changed, for we had knelt
beside him as he died, till Tom said: "If Leina were here she would say, 'Thank God!'
and I will say it for her. The mercy he sought
day and night this painful month came to him,
but at hell's margin."

We were sacredly affected by Tom's words,
but could not help the trill of amusement that
mingled with our shock of awe at his emphatic

caution in giving thanks. We often noticed that he always liked to have his wife between him and the Great White Throne. The brave, warm, large heart felt safest that way. He knew that the throne had no controversy with her; that she was secure in its presence. But himself? Well, the readers can see him for themselves, for he was sincere and true as light is bright.

Life has its mysteries; death his. And this was strange to me—the dying young man's despair for a ruined life, wrapped in the death-sleep, awakened by whom? His mother, he said, who had died a year before across the continent, and hymned to him of Jesus in the valley of the shadow of death as he bordered hell till in the triumph of hope and peace he escaped to heaven.

A few friends gathered from the cañons, and we buried him in a hollow of the mountains where the attrition of ages may cover him deeper and deeper; but the everlasting hill shall yield him up when Christ shall bid him rise.

CHAPTER IV.

YOU TRAMPLE FRAGMENTS OF GOLD.

N those days persons in the mines were seldom known except by a sobriquet; and often friends met who had been many years separated without recognition. But one day, when Hal S.'s comrade—Van—was able to sit up he caressed a picture, and said: "Her beauty cannot vanish. It derives from the heart more than from form and feature."

Tom barely glanced at the picture before he exclaimed: "Ella H.! It was ten years ago when I met her last, and then in Berlin; thence to Rome, she said."

"About that time," he replied, "I crossed the Mediterranean from Cairo, meeting her by arrangement at Florence; and amid its statuary and paintings she and I were made one. In our Pennsylvania home, training our little girl, she bides my return from the gold-fields."

The picture had revealed them to each other; and in the light of its dreamy eyes they remembered that they had been boys together, though more than a score of years had mapped their faces with cares since then. After this many a whimsical tale, sparkling with pranks, laughed their painful wounds into health again. The crags, the dumb rocks, the sunshine turning "somersets" in the air, the leaping river, the singing spring, the whistling quail in the jungle, seemed to share their joy.

What a blessed elf is childhood! It is fresh evermore. While the wild flowers tangle our feet along the school-path winding among fluttering birds and chattering squirrels, it stores in the depths of the heart soft memories to float up and come to light and joy life, when hard years have clustered griefs about us and stripped hope of all its winsomest myths. No marvel the sublime Christ loved to be in its circles with hand and voice of blessing only, and painted from it the sheeniest, sweetest picture of the many immortelles which illustrate the wisdom that comes down from heaven.

Though separated when boys, the education of Rothleit and Van had been matured in the German schools. Each had traveled Europe, and Van had been advantaged by a commercial residence of a few years at Cairo, the mart of the Nile. Yet he had not succeeded as a merchant, and Tom was, wonderful to tell, a self-confessed failure as a lawyer. But here, among the gnarled Sierras, Van had amassed several thousand ounces of gold; and a few months after he and Tom were thrown together he arranged to return home by "the next steamer."

Tom's accumulations were balanced by a few pennyweights; but, fascinated by the gold-phantom still, he strove to arrest his friend's homeward purpose. For he said to him: "Why go home with little more than a hundred thousand dollars, while here, wherever you walk, you trample fragments of gold as one does granite-flags on the Philadelphia pavements? Wait till at least a million of dollars crumples in your pocket as a bank-check."

Van's eye swept the vast area of rocks as he replied: "Fragments of gold, where? [Here are huge jumbles of rocks that appear to have been chipped by the gods off a hidden world while polishing it into symmetry and dumped on these chasms and peaks; but the gold?"

"Under them, under the *rocks*," said Tom, "or clasped in their hearts, are tons of gold. The gods covered it so as to test man's pluck. A few lucky strokes and it envelopes him in splendors like a world of meteors."

"That's a dream," Van replied. "The gold-phantom wove it of gold shreds and everlasting mountains of granite; and in the gleams of the infinitesimal shreds you forget that the mountains of adamant must be ground into dust before the shreds are yours. Whether by pearls of the sea or gems of the hills life is tissued, it is brain and muscle force, irksomely plied, that weaves the rich plaid. The castles that the gold-phantom builds are beautiful, but their bright blocks are only the jewels of a dream. Once as I journeyed the sea misty twilight built upon the waves a city of cloud-palaces. The work was done in a few minutes. They rose like magic creations upon the deep. Azure, purple, gray, golden, many-colored, they stood up upon the sea like castellated wonders of materiality. But they were but gorgeous vapor molded into temples and homes, unique, charming, that a sigh of Zephyr in a moment dissolved. Such castles does the gold-phantom build. They are phantasies; they pass away like the city of vapors. They are not habitable. No tenantry develop their domains; they yield no rentals. Not a fruit nor a flower ripens or unfolds in their borders. No child-voice breaks with cheery sound upon the silent mystery holding court there. They never echo a footfall, the merry ring of laughter, nor

the brawny thud of labor. They are exquisite
nothings that shine only when the sun —common sense—dips to sleep in the rustling waves
of actuality. Leave the phantasm. Its lures
are spread here upon peak and plain like a
sky of wonders, and many are the eagles it
snares till they pine away and die. Return to
the Atlantic Slope with me. Cling to law. Its
toils are adapted to you; those of mining are
not."

Tom appeared to be astounded—as he told
me afterward—by the supreme folly of the
argument, and seemed never to have heard any
thing so absurd as the proposal with which it
concluded; and said in reply, in a sort of hopeless, jerky, rhapsodic way: "Can't; can't think
of it. Borrowed gold to come to the gold-
fields; am borrowing gold to gather the gold
scattered all over them to pay back. Broke!
Return to the Atlantic States! go to nothing
with nothing and be nothing forever! Impossible! Tired—of law—to death. I want to rest.
It hardens nature. Wrecked a heart and fortune by it—somehow. Must recuperate. I
shall soon 'strike it rich'—unveil a gemmed
vault of incalculable deposits among these
rocks. Stay with us, Van, and share the pro-
digious quantity of gold we shall gather."

"Do, Van," said I. "The quantity already is 1 with a period preceding, followed by a world of ciphers, to which we shall soon add, by Tom's showing, a Jupiter full of units on the left. Stay."

Said Tom, rather pertly, I thought: " I discovered in old Zach's Mexican campaign that an army surgeon had little practical sense except when extracting bullets from dead soldiers or ordering one to be buried. My *arguments* are unanswerable, as Van knows. We cannot fail to unearth a cave full of gold in less than a month's time. Van, stay. We 'll third it with you, and add half a ton to your part."

An incredulous smile rippled Van's face as he shook his head and discerned how hopeless the effort to break the phantom's spell on Rothleit.

CHAPTER V.

AS THOUGH FURIES WERE IN THEM.

HEN morning flooded the jungle with light we watched Van from our camp climbing along the abrupt face of the mountain by the perilous trail, buoyantly rising— now visible, now hidden—two thousand feet, scaling the height, "going home." An eagle to his right gyrated from a sun-bright crag perpendicularly up higher and higher in the unflecked ether till—a speck, a moment on quivering poise—it fell spirally down, down, like a gray bolt of shimmering steel, and flashed its pinions in our eyes, between him and us, as it swooped athwart the drear abyss and perched upon the ragged crest of an opposite crag. We hailed the brave bird with a wild shout, for we felt the fourth of July leaping from peak to peak in fetterless liberty as its defiant swoop up, down, athwart the cañon, on high again, caught our eyes and snatched us to our feet. As we intently watched it, it dropped over on helpless wing, sprawling, tumbling,

falling a thousand feet into the dismal gorge. The puff of smoke that whiffed up just beyond its aerie told us that a hunter with fatal aim had pierced the shining mark. In a few moments we beheld him standing where the eagle had stood, peering into the abyss, and we almost wished to see him too topple from the height. But he cautiously drew away from the frightful brink.

Van had paused on the farther summit beyond the river, viewing like a spelled artist the cragged scenery by which we were interlocked, painting on his brain each wonder that nature here was lifting to the clouds upon her chasmed bosom. He was obviously aware that at his altitude he appeared like a dwarf to us, for he bent to the ground to make sure to our sight his last salutation, and passed out of sight forever, we thought, round the white dome of the snow-capped Sierra.

As we stood gazing toward the space whence Van had disappeared, our attention was attracted by the sound of a panther-like tread coming from the mouth of the gloomy rift next to us. Presently the intertwining shrubbery noiselessly opened, and the huntsman stepped—rather glided—out upon the narrow plateau we occupied. He greeted us courteously, and appeared

3

to be about thirty years old. His bearing be-
tokened one used to cultured life; yet even a
casual glance descried a fugitiveness in his eye
and a lynx-like gleam in his placid, beardless
face that indicated, amid seeming virtues, a
shrewd guile capable of little or monstrous
trickery. Such was his tact and demeanor,
however, that the unwary would as soon look
for poisonous fangs in a dove's beak as for el-
ements of the miscreant in him. He spent a
chatty hour with us, and inquired, *en passant*,
after Van, stating that he had heard that he
wished to sell a mining claim; and he went
from us across the pathless mountain southward.

The next day the mule-back expressman had
barely left us to our " letters from home" when
we were startled by the return of Van, looking like an apparition from Dante's gloomy
hell. His usually joyous, animated face was
impassive, pale, haggard, drear, hard. His
lips were compressed as if his teeth were
ground into one another. His eyes were
gleamy, dilated, fixed, yet appearing as though
furies were in them. His form at brief intervals shook as though convulsed by resistless
electric shocks. His air was that of frenzied
desolateness. And his voice, when at last we

heard it, was discordant, harsh as hate, yet strangely mournful. We grasped his hand, but it gave no return pressure. It was dry, hot, nerveless. And he leaned against the tent-post like a form of marble. He apparently heard nothing, uttered nothing, noticed nothing, replied to nothing; appeared unconscious of creation around, looking fixedly, fiercely into some fathomless horror on creation's verge.

To me the interview was intolerable. The picturesque spot whereon we stood, the songful spring near, the whizzing river; the gray, rent, huge rocks; the blue ravines; the humming forests; the ether-robed mountains; the majestic heavens—every object seemed to image him in horror's confounded amaze, and to press him chilled yet afire to my very being. My own brain began to seethe; my teeth clinched; my blood leaped, paused, then bounded crazily again; my heart stood still, then beat in convulsions; my senses were numbed. The abyss, the eternal hills, the heavens, whirled around, and, whirling me, seemed to totter, topple, tumble together in the supernatural gyration. I felt that my eyes too and face were taking on that strange look like his; that I was going crazy, I almost

shrieked with the frenzy. Had I been Job I
could not have prayed then for my friend; had
I been "a son of Belial" I could not have
cursed his foe. For my whole nature seemed
to have been transmuted into the condition
of horror that Van's wrong, whatever it was,
had thrust upon him.

Rothleit possessed an inexplicable virtue;
men leaned upon him at once in trouble—they
trusted in him. He appeared unconscious of
the quality, yet it sat as chief in the armies of
his heart till distrust confided to him and despair clung to him with the sense of rescue
and relief. Remembering this, I turned aside,
leaving him alone with Van, who, I hoped,
would speak to him if I were gone. But I
paused near—to interfere on occasion—in a
group of marble busts chiseled by the tempests; for a rankling dread that Van would kill
him had seized me. Van soon tossed a letter
to him, upon which his glance had fallen but a
moment ere he shook it from him as he would
an adder, and, with a fierce exclamation, sprung
to his feet. But quickly he was quiet as the
Sea of Galilee stilled by Jesus, and read the
letter as though its contents were the veriest
commonplace. Lifting his eyes from it to
Van, he said, "There is some mistake here."

"No," said Van.

"The statements must be false; the letter may be a forgery," he suggested in slow, calm tones.

Clutching the letter, he answered with hissing vehemence: "I tell you *no*. By every stroke of the pen I vow her own father wrote it. *She* is false. She!"

And his hand nestled like lightning on Tom's breast; and, holding him off at arm's length, his fiendish eye danced the reveille of the pit. But Tom very quietly said: "Impossible. Think. Her blood is without taint as far back as you can trace it. Indiscreet, *possibly;* not impure. Van, that's the worst of it."

"But," replied he, "at the trading-post different persons from my section in the East have received similar statements in letters. Her marriage and flight to Australia are assured."

"Alas!" said Tom; "it is inexplicable. I don't believe it. When such a woman is involved it is wise to hope, just to wait time's light upon the mystery."

Van gasped and tottered. The surges of fiery passions had stricken him to the sward like lightning; and we bathed his brow and lips that seemed now sealed forever. The letter that had met him at the trading-post the

day before and turned his heart to flames was
from his wife's father, revealing her secret di-
vorce, then marriage and departure from New
York for Australia.

It was a sad sight, that mad struggle of the
stricken man with the demon insanity. And
one night as he raged bitterest in stark delirium the hunter came again, and craved lodging
till morning. As he sat watching with us till
a late hour, we noticed that when Van was
wildest, and uttered with maniac emphasis the
name of him who had eloped with his wife,
a flitting sneer glared on his face. And during the hours that he slept we observed that
his dark hair was a wig that, disheveled in
sleep, betrayed a suit of auburn hair more
properly his own. Next morning he spiced
our breakfast of quail that his skilled gunnery
had supplied with pleasant anecdotes, in which
military phrases were noticeable, and, as he
bid us good-by, said: "If Van dies, please
announce it in the Sacramento dailies. I will
watch for it."

For several days sleep forsook Van's eyelids. He was fiercely alive, yet dead to every
thing save the disclosure concerning his wife.
That coiled about his being like a serpent of
fire, wringing him in its burning folds till his

eyes glowed in their sockets like focused per-
ditions. The thought *home* enraged him inde-
scribably. Before the horror befell he built
upon it many joyful anticipations, traced to
it many delightful memories, and constantly
spoke of it with exceeding pleasure. And the
bright morning he parted with us to journey
to it he appeared like one in an exultant trance;
but ere noon had come he wished the hours
were forever that kept him away from it.

Home. How exquisitely pleasing the trains
of feeling that bound through the heart when,
among strangers and distant scenes, the soul
trances the separating spaces and rests in its
borders again, and breathes the air and feels
the sunshine that huzzaed its childhood! But
it is essential agony to have the soul barred
against those richly freighted trains, their signals unheeded; their puff, puff of kindly approach disregarded; its palace darkened by the
black smoke rising from the heart burning up
itself; its ears noting not a pleasant melody in
all the joyful sprites that make home the music of life; only the paining chorus of the fiery
agony is heard by it evermore—day, night,
rain, shine—as crisper and more charred the
burning heart becomes. And this was Van's
condition now.

We alternated in watching by his side, yet it was so often that our united strength was required to control him that one day we fell asleep at the same time from insupportable weariness. When we awoke Van was gone. We traced him to a huge rock that, like a basking Gorgon, stretched boldly out into the river, compressing its floods into a narrow, down which they rushed in spiteful shrieks, fretted by the jagged channel into bounding billows. Opposite the rock's point grew a willow that bent over the rapids, vainly striving to rest its quivering boughs upon the rock. Several branches had been freshly torn from it, and itself was wet, as though beast or man had leaped from the rock into its slender limbs in a wild struggle to cross the boiling waters, and had been lost in the attempt. We could not trace our friend from that spot. From neither side did any foot-print guide away. And after days of painful search we concluded that he had been beaten to death by the maddened rapids upon their granite bed, and tossed derisively on to the far-off tule-quags, to sleep in their mystic hush forever.

CHAPTER VI.

HEART YEARNED FOR THE RIFLES TO HUSH.

HORTLY after we had lost Van an old comrade of his found the way to our placer. I first beheld him on the mine's brink observing Roth at work. As he caught my glance he said: "I would like to be his partner. He dreams gold, I know, and believes that every next pry of the pick will break into a tentful of it.'

Roth greeted him in the same humor, and we sauntered up to the camp. He appeared to have but one real anxiety—nót to own gold long. Yet he labored with energy for it. It obtained, he got rid of it with sunny indifference. He kept it busy by "staking,'' as he called it, every broken miner he met; and, considering that most miners kept themselves broke, he "had a time of it." He spoke Spanish and French, and wrote each accurately, having been educated in New Orleans and brought into habitual association with persons

using those languages. His adventures among
the Comanche Indians and in the war with
Mexico had imparted to him an air of melancholy, with physical and intellectual dash and
self-reliance. A few weeks' mining on this
placer made his pocket very like our own—
empty—not because of its outflow, but for lack
of inflow. Yet he lounged of evenings in the
purplish halo that lolled down between the
mountains as carelessly as though the reverse
was true. We were not so complacent, and I
disturbed the quiet of the camp one day by
announcing the purpose to take to the mountains with pick and pan and prospect for richer
diggings.

Roth only lifted his eyes above the distant
snow-peaks mournfully. Mack, supine on the
ground, his head pillowed on a rock, his rubber-booted heels stuck as high up a hemlock-
tree as he could get them, made no sign, only
he puffed a whiff of smoke sheer up among
the boughs and watched it thinning, floating
higher and vanishing like a phantasy in thin
air. Then he whiffed upward other puffs, with
long pauses between. Presently he tossed his
pipe after the smoke and said: "Prospect!
I've prospected from San Diego to Yreka and
back this far. I'm a-weary of it. I'll wait

here until a huge nugget trips me up, then I—will—pick it up—may be, and be rich enough to turn Tom's air-castles into realities when he comes back broke down and mournful as that donkey out there. I shall wait here." ·

"Wait!" exclaimed Tom. "Wait is the thriftless child of laziness, and industry has not the folly to dally with it. I go with Quien."

"You are a logician, Tom," rejoined Mack. "Seneca discovered the riches of poverty in the light of his jeweled table, and, extolling its blessedness, was no less consistent than you. You have dinned 'wait, wait' into our ears so long that we call this the 'Wait Mine.' And now you would have us think that they who wait are atypic grunts of humanity, adipic sloughs on the waves of progress, 'deads' on the veins of toil that thrill the world. Verily, not to swear, they who wait are pompous, puffed, poor, fond swells, pouring saturnalia upon the pure currents of brain and muscle that dignify man. Beshrew the dank bloats! Rich, poor, placid, low—let them uncoil, get to something, prospect, or their friend Lucifer will make them thralls to do *his* bidding. But I will wait for all that; the 'Wait Mine' is mine."

As his cool, tantalizing tones ceased he indeed looked like he would wait till the death-sigh of time. But presently a large bear waddled without a thicket, and ascending a bluff looked curiously down at us. We watched his queer observations till he prowled off into a jungly gulch.

"Let him go prospect," said Mack;" "he'll return, for Tom is the fattest nugget he can find. He will come back for him."

He was barely silent when the bear came in view again and squatted on the bluff. He stepped into the tent, passed to Tom a rifle, shouldered another, and, nodding to bruin, they wheeled silently into the chaparral. They soon gained a covert in fifty paces of the bear, who the next moment leaped high into the air and fell over the marble ledge into the whirling rapids. Only Roth had fired, had missed the mark, and Mack, uttering a jubilant shout, stood leaning on his rifle gazing on the affrighted beast as he struggled in the fretted current, and near the tent came ashore, disappearing in the gorge that here opened its dark mouth to the tortured floods. When they had returned, Roth said to Mack: "Why didn't you shoot him as he was swimming? You had a dozen opportunities ere he was beyond bullet-range."

"I know it," Mack replied; "but I could not shoot. When I was a boy I went with some Texan Rangers to flush a band of Co-manches. They ambuscaded us. The two soldiers who escaped the massacre with me were slain the following night as we huddled around a few coals in a tempest. I again escaped in the thicket. The next day, worn, weary, fevered, hungry, I stood, as the sun was setting, upon a bluff washed by a swollen river. It had stormed all the day. As I looked up and down the stream to detect some means of crossing, a volley of bullets whistled by my head and heart. I leaped far out into the rushing flood, and swam and dived and plunged amid bullets and arrows to the flat swamp opposite. How my heart yearned for the rifles to hush, for the arrows to whiz no more! When the bear turned his somersault into the river, I remembered that incident. How could I shoot him? I felt that he was me scringing, plunging in the water with a heart-wail for life. About midnight a sense of safety came over me, and I stopped in the darkness, stood upon my head, walked upon my hands, feet up, and played 'turn the wheel' in the young cane, and wished to yell with delight at my escape. But a racket to the right scared

me, and I glided on till daylight showed me
the plains. I had scarcely entered upon them
when I heard my father's whistle of danger in
a ravine. I fled toward it as a bullet cut
the grass under my feet. Then another rifle
cracked, and I heard a groan near me, and
glancing back saw a Comanche rising and falling, but he was still ere I reached my father,
whose aim had been sure. Bruin is safe. I
rejoice with him. And Roth, when you fight
a duel—that men about your caliber are sometimes not wise enough to avoid—see that your
enemy is as good a shot as yourself; then neither will spill blood. You missed the bear a
a foot or two at least. I was sure you would
do so when I nudged you as you were aim-
ing."

"So you jostled me as I shot of purpose," laughed Tom; "I thought so at the
time."

"Yes; and huzzaed when your bullet flat-
tened on a rock to the bear's right," replied
Mack.

The next day Roth and I, with a brown donkey, were threading a rough-visaged route
prospecting. Summits conic, truncated, symmetrical, ragged; snow-crowned peak kings
that the shocks of many seasons had not dis-

crowned, with gloomful abysses between, and vast shadows lengthening, widening, darkening about them like mystic creations, marshaled about our pathless course.

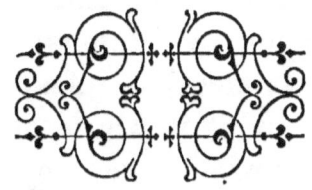

CHAPTER VII.
THE DEAD MAN'S GHOST.

HE third week of our prospecting trip brought us—many miles from our starting-point—high up on Dead Man's Creek that pushed its snow floods in leaps from ledge to chasm, over bowlder and pebbled channel, in shout and hiss, and murmur and splash, as though a regiment of school-boys were rollicking in its pools and falls. Great rocks locked to the bluffs by columnar links of granite overhung its depths. And bleak crags grouped close about it whose shadows darkened it. We knew not that any one was in a day's journey of the solitary place, and we pitched camp for the night.

I was very tired; Tom said I was always so; and he was very blue. We sat upon the bank thirty feet above the stream watching the isinglass glisten on the rocky bottom; and he was delighting me, he thought, by describing to me the hundredth time his wife and children. Tom—his namesake—he said, was the image of himself; but I could see by the pictures that he was just the reverse—very like his mother; and desiring a change of subject, I dropped a nugget, and managed that his eye should catch its glitter in the water. He attempted vainly to make me see it too; so he scrambled down to the pool where it lay laughling at its owner; for the beautiful specimen was his own. Many miles away, and several months before, he had pried it from a crevice and given it to me to keep till he could send it home. But such was his exultation that he knew it not. Hope's reactionary gas fairly sparkled in his face and crackled in his leaping voice as he secured it and held it up for my inspection.

"I 'll prospect awhile," he said; and the rapid thuds of the pick told me he was at work under the bluff. And I rejoiced that he had found something else to do besides to talk. He loved to talk; and I had learned to think and dream dreams or make elaborate calculations amid his most charming bursts of talk, not noting a word he said. But it was all the same to him so *he* talked, for it never entered his mind to conceive so preposterous a thing as that any one could be otherwise than raised into nearly divine raptures by the music and

4

wisdom of his words. After awhile I called him repeatedly, but could get nothing of him but "wait." So I concluded to break up his business. A few yards from the spot where he toiled were rents in the bluff, and thrusting a pole into one of them, several tons of rubbish lumbered to the bottom. He uttered a wild yell as the avalanche broke loose, and fled, leaping through the creek as if an earthquake were after him. I hurried to the camp and busied about supper. In a few minutes he came to the camp, and, girding a blanket about him, hung his clothing to the fire to dry. In answer to my query, "What's the matter, Tom?" he replied: "O nothing! nothing— much; I just stepped into the creek—a—little."

I had a notion about the "just stepped" and the "a—little;" but he brought to me his pan, and in the gleam of the ounce and more of gold his hour's work had unearthed we forgot the incident.

That night the moon put on her shiniest robes, and laughed in the heavens in a glee of glory. The wilderness was like a silvery illumination. A wolf now and then trotted across the purple haze of our camp-fire, and a frightened deer leaped past. Besides these, nothing disturbed the splendid solitude save the moon-beams shattering on woods and rocks and the muffled sighs of the dreamy wind. True, Dead Man's Creek murmured in our ears refrains of the murdered man whose corpse named it; but we transmuted the doleful melodies into golden anthems, and, soothing our loneliness in the hopeful chorus, fell asleep to rhythms of imagination sweeter than Orpheus struck from his golden shell. For fancy whispered to us wonderful things concerning much goods laid away in store by the daughters of gold waiting for us among the rocks and cascades under the bluff.

About midnight Tom awoke me, whispering in my ears: "There's the dead man's ghost groaning and muttering right across the creek, keeping watch on us."

I doubt if a battle of thunder-storms could have stirred me sooner. And sure enough, thirty steps from us, a pale, distorted face glistened beside a quivering clump of manganite. Presently we traced the full outlines of the shape; for it was restless. It clutched the air, moaned, gnashed its teeth, but slept all the while it seemed, however anguished, muttering words of rage and murder. During the while Tom appeared dissatisfied with himself—uneasy—and strolled up the creek. In a few minutes I saw that he had crossed over and seated himself beside the fierce, pale sleeper. He touched him, shook him. He, waking with a drear roar, seized him, and a wild struggle to save life and to take it began. I knew not what to do. Ere I could possibly reach the crossing one or both would be dead. I screamed—but who heard me? In a few moments he darted to the precipice with Tom lifted in the air as if he were a cork to hurl him into the jaggy chasm, exclaiming: "Fiend! fiend! to hell with you!"

I knew the voice, and shouted, "Van!"

He drew back from the dismal brink, and said, "Quien."

And said I—pointing to Roth, whom he still held throttled—"Tom."

He laid him down tenderly, kissed his ashy face, and wrung his hands in agony over him. Hurrying to the crossing, I soon gained the scene of the rencounter; but they were gone. I peeped into the dank chasm, but heard nothing save the splash of the fretted waters. But from along the mountain-side over me sounds like staggering footsteps fell upon my straining ears, and I sped after them, thinking that Van's frenzy had returned, and that he was scaling the crag with Tom to hurl him, in prankish madness, from its moon-lit height into the awful gorge that yawned at its base like a bottomless hell. Now and then a stone loosened by his ascent bounded down by me as the leaves and twigs rustling beneath his tread guided my pursuit. Five minutes that seemed an hour intervened ere I overtook him under Tom's dead-weight pressing, straining up the mountain; and, laying my hand upon his shoulder, said: "Put him down, down!"

But he leaped away from me with a wail, and with mad strength and agility climbed on up the crag's face, over log and rock and fissured gorge. And still above and just beyond him I heard the groaning of a water-fall as it fell ceaselessly over a glum precipice, and its white face gleamed like pale death waiting for us. I tripped him, and, as he rolled twenty feet down the steep, wrested Roth from his eager clutch, and ere he regained my side was laving his dead face at the basin of the water-fall. He stood by me speechless, watched with awed eagerness each manipulation, stooped, peered into my eyes, touched the ashy-pale face, and whispered, "Dead?"

"No; not yet," I replied.

And silent, quick as thought, he plunged

into the boiling flood with him—across, up, and away with him—with a frantic yell, toward a cliff that gleamed like a grand dome near the summit. But he sunk to the ground in a few minutes, exhausted by the contrary frenzies that had surged in his soul and by his burdened, reckless rush up the height.

I again knelt over Roth. His pulse fluttered and was still. His heart trembled, then went to sleep. But as we rubbed and called him the pulse leaped and was at rest again; the heart throbbed, was lost to motion, throbbed, throbbed, throbbed. Tom sighed and sat up. Van's eye danced delightedly, and he stretched himself beside him, limber as a molten form; but the pathetic "Thank God!" he uttered told me he was in his right mind.

Roth looked from one to the other, felt his wet garments, touched the blood upon them softly, inquisitively, and said: "What *does* it all mean?"

"It means," I replied, "that you are yourself the stark fool forever, been fighting 'the dead man's ghost,' who flitted up here with you, and went in a-washing with you as he came by the falls. Could n't you have let the haunt alone? Why have you gone over there to disturb it?"

A wave of happy humor rippled Van's face, and he knelt up in the moonlight by Tom, who, with boy-like joy, recognized him, and said: "So *you* are the ghost. Well, I was—scared a —some, I think, and am hurt a little; but it's nothing. I would go through it again to find you."

And so he would have done. Indeed, had he been Dante among the infernals, instead of storing his brain with their horrors to detail in a book, he would have turned himself into a cinder trying to loose the fired devils.

We helped him up the peak to a cliff on its side that appeared in the moonshine like a castle of silver. In its heart was Van's cave, whither he was hurrying Tom when I overtook him. There we bestowed him on a bed of grizzlies' skins, and, leaving him asleep, we walked out upon the promontory that jutted sheerly from the crown of the height athwart an abyss whose depths, like the mythic river of sighs, were hidden in fathomless dark.

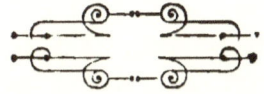

CHAPTER VIII.
GRATINGLY ATHWART THE PEAK'S FACE.

HE scene was wondrous. The stupendous rocks; the zigzag spurs bald, wooded; the solitary peaks snow-robed in solemn valleys; the piled ranges leaning against the star-lit horizon drooping its glittering circle on every side; the hoarse calls of the winds; the sough of the vast waste; the moan of the drear abyss; the whispers of pale ether worshiping between earth and sky, imparted to the heart a delightful awe.

Van appeared to be oblivious of the scene, intent on peering far beyond. A river, tossing its floods amongst far-away Atlantic hills, held upon its bosom his memories and his dead hopes, and he was floating now upon its far-off current. His heart had tranced the continent to swim upon its waves with the ghosts of the past, and as one and another of them glided to the surface he voiced the thoughts they evoked.

"Life was sweet as peace then," he said.

"Bright as joy. Hope smiled. Miriam was the ideal of loveliness; our little girl was fair to look upon. I prospered. Misfortune befell in the course of years. My father passed away; my mother quickly crossed the cold stream after him to God's shore. Debts came to light—mortgages dusty with age. And to redeem the old homestead I hurried to these gold-fields. But the sacred prize is blurred by the naked woe that grew in its soft shadows, hushing for all time the spirits of joy in its groves and halls while it was being redeemed with gold gathered here. Redeemed! Alas, it is lost! Not all the jewels of the Sierras can light it with smiles again for me. Why did I come hither? Fatal land, death-place of all sunny dreams, shall I thank you for gold? It is but fine dust in the balance against the happiness it costs. Why did I come to thy dizzy heights and dreamy valleys? Yet these silent glories have not injured me. The horror was born elsewhere. At home its wail arose, and leaped a continent to damn me while hurrying there to look upon the fairest picture in all the world to me. The picture? Marred. The joy? Fled. A life-woe born; home expunged from the soul. How? A *heart*, instead of sparkling at anchor in purity's ha-

ven, admits a profane feeling to dally with her
white wings, and waft her out upon the turbid
sea forbidden to pure voyagers. Can she be
recalled? The storms are black with fury
there. Spirits from the pit lash its waters.
In vain the heart lightens her load; the pilot,
innocence, is dead. She becomes stained like
the billows which toss her. She drives with
the tempest awhile. When she *would* return,
there is no way back for her from the black
sea she sails. Her signals of distress are
mocked by sailors on that main. Her lurid
rockets, unheeded by the safe ashore, die in
the thick night that shrouds her. No beacon
on rock shines for her. Beaten, shivered,
forsaken, adrift, in the swoop of the storm and
crash of breakers, she must sink in the inky
waters. She is lost. Only One is good enough
to throw a bow of promise athwart the dark
gulf, and great enough to sail a life-boat over
its boiling surf for her rescue. Will she heed
His promise and be found of him? God help
the poor voyager to Christ who stoops from
heaven to hell to save a soul! Lost?"

I stood shivering at his side, for he seemed
like a talking corpse, the stars bending from
above, the yawned abyss waked up from beneath, listening to him. Obviously, he was

oblivious of me and of every object about him. His form was rigid, not a muscle quivered, and his wide-open eyes stood still as his form, as his burning heart dropped out in words that hissed as they hid in the pale ether.

"Lost," he repeated. "Who is lost? A woman, gentle as love, trusting as faith, unsuspecting as hope, beautiful as chastity. She lost! Damned!"

His voice here was a whisper; yet it sounded to me like a lorn, stark shriek leaping over the icy Sierras from crag to cloud, to wilderness, to plain, to river, to city; across continents and seas—here, there, everywhere—seeking, like zigzag lightning, some certain object to fall upon. I imagined that Miriam, his wife, heard him in her hiding-place, and quivered, as I did, at the fiendism that irked and fired and shot out his last word like a hell in aspirate in quest of her. But *she* had no need to startle. The heart whose hot haste projected the measureless "damn" lodged no spite for her, yet excused her not while it pitied, but mourned her with a fiery mourning. He was still rigid, save that his eyes burned in the moon's glint as if a fury afire were in rhapsody in them as he continued: "Which is the perditionable? Man says, 'She is.' Man, glowing

with might and honor, ermined with justice
and mercy, says, 'She is the damnable one,'
and garlands him who hurled her from innocency; laureates the fiend, but whips his victim
forth into night. That's *his* justice, honor,
might, mercy—damning the *wronged*. Woman
says, 'She it is who is perditionable.' Woman,
like Christ, touched with the feeling of our
infirmities, beautiful, brave, loving, who be-
wailed the Christ in the face of spiteful hell,
adored at his tomb almost as early as the angels, and acclaimed his resurrection to Rome's
sneering savages and Jerusalem's crucifying
ingrates—*she* says that it is she that is beyond
pardon. She scouts her to the pit pitilessly.
She assigns her to eternal scorn, and hisses
her eternally. But him that beguiled her?
She smiles on him, welcomes him to hearth
and heart; weds him. Hiss him! Why?
What evil hath *he* done? Lured to perdition
only a woman. Shorn her of that grace that
makes her so like a heavenly visitant. Crushed
her good heart. Gloomed her life with the
abyss's night. Hiss him for that? Not so.
Kiss him rather, laud him, love him, wed him.
O sweet logic! Heaven for the devil, hell for
the victimated of his pestilent wickedness. O
sweet logic! The hell of humanity enlarges

its choicest Satan, and for the ruin he inflicts tortures woman with an infinity of anathema, and saints *him*."

The fierce sneer of his sentences entered in the soul, the vividest image of the intense outrage perpetrated against the beguiled in the given circumstances; an image that turned from her the merciless hates that beat her beneath the surf—turned them to their proper mark, the inexpressible wretch who pilots her into the sea of shame. They are *his*, not hers—*his*, fetidest corruption of humanity that he is.

Satan rubbed out the garden planted by God. Its fruits and flowers and trees, its tree of life, at his touch disappeared. And earth bristled with thorns as a testimony against him. But the man who blurs the heaven of woman's heart, and sends her strangling with woe to mate with fiends, is caressed in tribute of his victory, and welcomed into earth's sacredest bowers. Nature cries to heaven against the unnatural crime. The hurtling scorn should center upon the brute-beast man instead. It was after *him* that Van's jagged "damn" leaped. And the unspeakable pathos of his prayer that God would help *her* to Christ gave a fury to the naked lightning of the curse upon him that flamed like a bolt of doom. He had paused at the sentence, "Tortures woman with an infinity of anathema, and saints him;" his face paler than the dead, his haughty form quivering as in the throes of some tumultuous passion. But he quickly resumed, saying: "Ay, but beast sheltered by society, your infamy tinseled by the favor of those who, like the goddess truth, should spurn you farthest into the realm of reproach—your sin, *yours,* will find *you* out. God, who quietly moves when he will into your rankling circles, though panoplied by hosts in arms for you, will crush you as though you and they were veriest trifles. It is the Almighty who says, 'I will repay.' Your brassy heart, soon or late, must ring wails to the metal of his wrath. Two spirits commune with me. One urges to slay, slay *him.* And I often leap in sleep to grapple him, but to find it was only a phantasy of the brain I had met. To-night I thought Tom was he, and that retributive Nemesis had conveyed him to me that I should hurl him into pitiless death. Why am I here? Why not bounding in pursuit? The other spirit enticed me. Its voice is not for blood. It is a gentle thing, yet it braves revenge in his fiercest mood, and tells him he is a criminal of Satanic hue;

that to murder is monstrous. In the haunts
of men its voice is smothered. But here,
where all nature speaks of God, I hearken to
its pleadings. Not the eagle that rends, but
the dove traversed the deluge on good bent.
Close to the awful waves, adown their dank
chasms, over their glowering crests, in the
spray of their thunders, she sped, till, finding
the leaf of peace, she retraced her brave path
to the ark and trustingly fluttered against its
window for admission with the life-promise to
its inmates. So this gentle spirit has fluttered
about me in this horror. It allured me to
this wild. It induces me to seek rencounters
with beasts instead of man; to study the rocks
and plants; to hearken to the stars; to heed
God in the tumbling falls, the rustling forests,
the flashing avalanches, the quiet heavens—
ministers of his that do *his* pleasure. What
is it? It is gentle as the angel of mercy, and
mighty. It trips hell and hustles it from the
heart, but touches each delicate flower there
into softer, sweeter, lovelier mold. Is it God?
It is oft so utterly tender that I think it is my
mother come from the dead to quell with her
gentleness the fury that earth-wrongs have
stirred. Do departed spirits of the good come
to earth again, trace the way of mortals, min-

ister blessings? Who doubts it but a carnal-
ist sneering at divinities? But coming, why
invisible, without voice? Rather, do we not
hear them with the soul, spirit to spirit heed-
ing."

He looked away to the farther chasm—pale
above with moonlight, black below its jungle-
brow—up to the spangled sky, into the sheer
abyss at our feet, and reeled to a bust of glinty
quarts peeping above the granite like a Titan's
head, and sat upon it. There was a crazy
white flame in his eye that I could not read,
and the wide-eyed stars seemed to stoop down
to catch the expression of his face and to shiver, hearing words like fire from a man of ice
as he added: "Yet I often think it were happiness to drop off the height upon the rocks
in the abyss's fatal depths. Fearful images
wring my brain. Vengeance convulses me,
and gloats on a coming meeting with him
whose sin, dyed in woman's heart-break, shapes
before me like the bolt of fate to drop him into
perdition. Blood starts in the air, drips from
my hands, curdles at my feet."

Here he sprung to his feet as if pierced by
his last words, exclaiming: "What if I had
killed Tom for him to-night? Curse, curse
upon the serpent who has crazed me!"

His tones were jagged and hissing like hurtling aërolites falling. He shuddered. His face grew whiter like the essence of rage. His eye gleamed like a maddened beast's. He rolled upon the ground like a convulsed maniac. He screamed in fury, and frenziedly tore himself. He leaped away—as if in pursuit of some one—from ledge to ledge, down from gorge to gorge, unconscious of friendship's or danger's presence—a poor, wildered, frantic wretch. And sky and jungle held their breath in an ecstasy of alarm as the raving specter bounded from the crag into the shadow of death.

As he skipped like a pale ghost out into the chasmy darkness, Tom, drawn to the spot by his mad exclamations, stood on the verge of the promontory, his face puffed by the night's throttling. He leaned over into the weird gloom, and from its depths a shriek, like a tiger's raging scream, leaped up and passed gratingly athwart the peak's face, and died in the sky.

"Not dead!" he gasped. "Good heavens! Come." And adown the peak, picking the way rapidly, swinging over from rock to rock, now tumbling, leaping here, sliding there; hesitating over a fissure, dropping in; scramb-

5

ling on down, we were soon buried in the abyss searching everywhere for Van.

The day-break glowed in the east, the sunrise purpled deeper and deeper the horizon and tinted the ice-like skies with blent pink and orange; the fresh airs of morning trooped in merry waves over cañon and cliff, and puffed refreshing ether into every thing; star after star fell asleep in the damasked vault; and full-orbed day smiled in heaven and earth as if neither crime nor horror, nor aught save purity and peace, had ever tossed about in the lap of time.

CHAPTER IX.

HE'LL LEAP, LEAP—LOST!

HE day passed in a hapless search for Van. So, leaving him to his fate, we built a brush tent in a group of nutmeg-trees, and mined in a cramped placer on the creek. Several days had elapsed when, weighing our gold, we had many ounces to jewel our girdles. We were wakeful the following night with exulting hopes. It was moonless, but the stars held levee, and we watched their glittering ranks arrayed in silvery robes as they passed and greeted and whispered and danced in the firmament, as if in a jubilee that restless earth soothed by Lethe lay dreaming. The midnight hour had sighed itself away, and still we were awake watching the pale love-flashes they exchanged, when a shrill whoop from far up the nodding crag that slept over us sprung us to our feet; and we peered up the abrupt steep to detect the fool-hardy adventurer essaying its descent. We could not distinguish him from many a shadowy appearance that

clung to its bald bust; but he evidently descried us in the glare of our camp-fire, for he
saluted our eager watch with a succession of
screeching yells that hideously echoed along
sky and chasm as he came down, down toward
us. Every few minutes stones or fragments
of turf fell from the gnarly crag into the muttering creek, when abruptly from a fissure a
hundred feet above us a form, clad—save boots
—like Adam before Eve fig-leafed him, glided
out upon a buttress and stamped in madness,
uttered a tempest of stark screams, and, leaning over, leered down upon us. The stars
seemed to float into groups over him, and to
hush their shuddering circles lest their rustling should startle him. Dead Man's Creek
muffled its lorn melody till each note was a
stifled sob, and the dark crag grew black with
awful horror that he recked not the peril.
Tom's ruddy face was aghast as he whispered:
'Van, Van, wild as the fiend! Watch. He'll
leap, leap—lost!'" And he glided into the
crag's shadow like a speeding specter, and I
noted him scaling its steeps toward him.

On diverting my eye again to the buttress,
Van was gone. I listened for a gnashing thud
in the creek, but heard nothing only Tom's incessant, quiet scramble up toward where he had

stood. While scringing round a protruding rock, he looked aloft and discovered that he had disappeared. He looked down, bent over, listened, looked to me. I motioned him on up, and watched thither, every nerve a tortured tremor, when, right at my ear, pealed, like a blast from the pit, a maniac "Ha, ha, ha!"

It tore my bones seemingly out of my flesh, and landed me a thousand feet from the spot, I hoped, but found that I had been so appalled as simply to fall in my tracks. And the madman's blazing eyes and furious grip told me death was near. I either heard, or thought I heard, Tom's groan of sympathy from the cliff's face, and, like impersoned fear, I kept Van too busy holding me for any chance to strike. About the first thing I remember after the struggle began is Tom upon Van's breast holding his right-arm and I kneeling on and lancing his left with dispatchful zest; and I was very thankful for my little knowledge of surgery. He bled refreshingly fast, I thought; and though his eyes were like globes of fire, and his struggles fierce, he weakened rapidly, and was soon in a faintish sleep, out of which I feared he would never awake. We dressed him in a ragged suit—best we had, part Tom's, part mine—and about day-dawn he woke up

with a feeble yawn. His recognition of us
was instant, and he tried to stretch out his
hand to greet us, but was too faint. He was
moody at intervals most of the day, but toward
evening he listened to a rehearsal of his last
night's pranks and perils, for he insisted till
we told him the worst; and ere night fell we
had packed him on the donkey by a circuitous
route up to his cave. He showed us therein
his cache of provisions and gold; and in the
gloaming, whose soft tints were nestling in the
dark between the crags, we spread down grizzlies' skins under the leafy nutmegs at its
mouth, and talked by snatches or dreamed
with open eyes the balmy hours far into the
solemn night.

"I have been alone here," he said, "three
months. The solitaire, as well as others, I
find, needs labor to relieve of unrest. Res-
pite or diversity is longed for. So I have
spiced solitude with toil. It rests the eye, the
mind, the muscles even. Sleep is sweeter,
and the wakeful day looks like a newer glory,
when labor makes merry music for the throng-
ing hours. The heart wrings out its sorrows,
and rings in hopes which delight it amid the
quiver and jostle of physical thuds. The
placer I am mining is but a short distance

above yours, and I have gathered among its crevices a fraction less than a thousand ounces. Unless you have done better, you must mine with me."

To this we acceded, and the days of the following month were golden for us. During the while Van was often restless, took sudden trips for days at a time into the sequestered jungle, and finally became resolute to voyage to Australia. Some phantasm on that distant shore seemed to call to him incessantly, and the vast stretch of sea between appeared at times but a step to him. And we remembered the letters had said that thither Miriam had been borne.

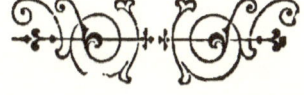

CHAPTER X.
MIRIAM THINKS, YES!

E appeared, of late, to be haunted by the image of his wife; and transient thoughts, like stray rays from angels, led him into glimpses of hope that some explanation existed that would condone her course and leave her to him as a pure memory at least. It was seldom, indeed, that he mentioned the trouble. But now and then he briefly spoke of it, and we, with bated speech, would suggest the pleasantest things possible germane to it. And so it became mingled with the camp talk one midnight and to little purpose, except to make him silent for a long interval after mentioning it. In his silence, sight too seemed to have repressed all her mysteries, and so to have hushed them that the soft step of a beast or man crept to us from a thicket a hundred paces distant and then was still so long we forgot it and became enthralled in reverie. But out of the strange hush·upon every thing there bounded to us a

short fierce roar, like that uttered by a savage in dire rage. It was followed by a furious rustling of the feathery boughs of the chaparral and hurried pistol-shots, and a dark body sprung from the covert across a broad bare rock and fell heavily upon the shrubs, thirty feet below its brink. In the instant a hatless man stepped to the rock's edge, and peered down as if anxiously watching some object. His form was distinctly outlined by the forest background and starshine, the pistol still gleaming in his hand. In answer to our hail, he said: "It is only a strange animal that disputed my passage through the jungle, where I have been wandering all day. It hurt me but little, and is past injuring any one now. I wish it had fled. I'm sorry I killed it."

It was Mack from the "Wait Mine." And Van, laughing, said: "Well, I'm glad it is quiet at least, for its scream made my pate grate as though some savage ghost had torn off its scalp."

Mack let himself down the rock's face by clinging to its wrinkles, and we examined the symmetrical brownish California lion he had slain, while he related how fortunately his first bullet arrested its arrowy leap upon him, when so near his person that its contortions rolled it against him as he repeatedly fired till it desperately plunged from him over the rock.

He and Roth lingered near the lion when Van and I returned to the camp. And when presently they followed us, an unusual animation was noticeable in Roth. Mack zestfully partook of the supper we hurriedly prepared for him; and leading the camp chat into good news from home, said quite naturally: "Van, I met awhile back a young man some twenty years old in San Francisco just from the Atlantic States. He claims to be your brother Will, and says that a letter from Roth to some one near your home in the East had led him to come to the gold-fields to meet you. He went on to the trading-post where you and Roth first met in this country, hoping there to get tidings of you. He said your wife was well except being heartsick to see you, and your little Miriam is as beautiful as the bird's song is sweet."

During the last statement Van had risen to his feet and had leaned against the huge rock next the cave, one hand clasping his heart; and in his eyes shone the eagerness that one in a desert ready to perish would likely feel if near him living waters should suddenly murmur. But Mack, seeming not to notice the intense posture, added: " We arranged a plan of communication, and two weeks ago he had turned this way on Roth's path. He says *all* is well at home. The old place redeemed by your remittances is all your own; and that in it has been waiting and longing for you, all the weary months of your absence, as noble a woman, as true a heart to you, Van, as ever pulsed deathless love. *The letters* to parties on this coast *are base forgeries."*

There Van stood mute, motionless, slightly leant toward Mack; only the flush of face and awing eagerness of his eyes tokened life. And Mack continued, his tones tremulous and clear with faith's passion in the words: "He asked me to say to you, if I should meet you before he did, that by the kindred blood which warms his heart, you may rely upon this statement as pure truth; that aught adverse to it is utterly, *utterly* false."

There was a quiver in Van's frame; he looked squarely into Roth's face, now suffused with tears as well as unusual animation, and the old classmates bounded together.

"And that's not all, Van," said Tom, as they resumed their places in the bear-skins. "Will has married Miriam's sister, and she and Miriam are in Sacramento with their father, vowing to kill you on sight."

"Is it so, Mack?" sharply queried Van.

"Yes," Mack answered quite dryly, "except the vowing."

"Well," said Van, "killing is a greater favor than my injustice to Miriam merits. But, Tom, I never revealed to you and Quien the evidence of the story's truth that was to me the convincing witness. It is Miriam's own letter avowing the affair and tearfully resigning to me our little girl. The style and chirography are so entirely her own that to doubt its genuineness never occurred to me until now.

The hours tripped away unnoticed, for we were happy in the peace that had come to Van, who, in its quieting melodies, entertained us by the rarest conversational powers within formation and incidents so foreign to himself and scenes about us that we forgot that sorrow had ever cast a shadow on his life.

The morning broke upon us while we were yet awake, and its sunrise sung us to sleep. We were roused by an old pioneer and his young comrade, upon whom Van's eyes rested with caresses as he greeted him with, "God bless you, Will!"

Will had collected; at the trading-post near our first mine, two or three of the forged letters, and we compared them with those Van had cached with his gold. The same hand was evinced in each, and those to Van, when compared to genuine letters, were so nearly perfect imitations that even the expert could scarcely have rejected them.

"Van," queried Will, as Van folded the letters and put them aside, "whose treachery is it? Think you, brother, that Lieutenant W. can have become so utterly vile as this? Miriam thinks, 'Yes.' He threatened vengeance the hour your marriage in Florence was known in America. Her brother, you remember, gave you notice of it while you were yet in.Europe."

"But," rejoined Van, "he met us on our return with many pleasant expressions of good feeling, and often as we were together nothing to the contrary appeared. He removed with his large fortune, within the year, to his home in England, and I never heard if he ever came back to America."

"When I was a boy," said Will, "I thought him glorious, and remember well his splendid equipage and fine person and manners; his hazel eyes and light curly hair, too, are in mind. Dr. P. once berated him for his mockery of the poor, and said his heart was a hyena's, while his mien was a lion's. I know that the old did not trust him, with all his fair

seeming. And I have heard your old college
chum, Col. F., say that he was a heartless
flirt, and base in resentments, equal to garland
with favors those he had designs upon till they
trusted him, while using others to bring them
annoyance; that Italian revenge is honor to
the masked cruelties his heart is base enough
to execute. He certainly loved Miriam; and
though you smiled at his rivalry, you dreaded
lest his artfulness should supplant you; so
at least F. used to say. And Miriam used
to say that he could bide a life-time to find
advantage to gratify a grudge."

"Where is Col. F.?" Van inquired.

"In Germany, when last heard from," he replied. "And at the time the forged letters
state he and Miriam were married, *his* marriage with Lieut. W.'s elegant cousin, Miriam,
was celebrated, and they took steamer for the
Old World. W. had been invited to the marriage, but excused himself on the plea that he
was about to sail for Africa on a hunting ex-
cursion of months."

"The wretch!" exclaimed Roth; "he was on
this coast four months ago. He it must have
been, Quien, who killed the eagle the morning
Van left our camp for home, and came down
into the fissure inquiring for him; whose light

curly hair appeared under his black wig when it was awry the night he lodged with us; and went back across the mountains to the trading-post, where, no doubt, he had personally repeated the forgeries of his infamous letters. You called my attention to his military style and phrases."

I cannot word-paint the expression in Van's face when Roth's disclosures followed the presumptions of Will. But any one beholding it would say that a meeting between him and W. would drop on the wings of the wind the heroic philosophy of self-repression in his promontory monologue, and reënact the scene of the moon-lit gulf, where Tom encountered him as the murdered man's ghost, and nearly lost his life for his wisdom.

With Will and the old pioneer he sped from the peaks toward the plains that afternoon, journeying to Miriam at Sacramento. No plea for rest could induce him to wait till next morning. Love's smoldering fire had returned at the altar of wifely honor, and by its witchery was causing him to leap like the hart to the presence of that unequaled enchantress—a pure, self-immolating, loving wife.

Mack remained to mine again with us.

CHAPTER XI.

THE PLAZA D'ARMAS QUIVERS.

NDUSTRY not being the special-
ty of either of us, as it had been
of Roth's forefathers, we could
promptly improvise a hunt or a
a ramble among the labyrinths
and mountains to inspect the stones and plants
and enjoy the beauties of leisure. In an ex-
cursion of that kind we were arrested, on a
rough summit, by a cracked voice in which the
"carrajo" of Mexico, the "sacre" of France,
and the abrupter profanity of the United States
were ludicrously intermixed. The voice approached us, then receded, and its mad jargon
left no doubt that its owner was terribly in
earnest about something. We glided a few
paces southward, and again heard its raving
imprecations. Presently the frantic jabberer,
with a hop and a skip, pranced along a beaten
path in thirty feet of the rocky clump in which
we were 'hidden. His eyes stood out with
fierceness; his long white hair, matted, flopped
about his face as he leaped on; and his cloth-

ing dangled in tatters about his stubby person. In a minute or two he rushed back muttering, his hands clasping several stones; and, turning behind a massive rock, we knew by his voice that he had stopped, and judged by the whiz and smash that he was stoning some object. We were soon in position to see his crazy work. Eight or ten paces from him, leaning against a large pine, was the motionless form of a bleeding Indian, with bow and arrows near him. The tree was barked in several places next his breast and cheek; and between throws the maniac, leaping up and down, screamed in the very ecstasy of rage. We were but little aside from the range of his devilish eye and its apparently dead object. As he hurled the last stone he galloped back in the path described, and Mack dashed to the lifeless Indian and bore him, with our aid, across a ravine into a tangle of young firs, where we were scarcely concealed ere the maniac was at his post again with another supply of stones. Dropping them at his feet, retaining one, he drew back to hurl it, when he was transfixed with surprise that his victim was gone. Now his manner wholly changed. He crouched and crept slowly, softly to the tree, came down upon his hands and knees,

6

and wormed himself with unspeakable caution peeringly round it, sprung to his feet
aghast, and sped away noiseless as a shadow,
exerting every muscle to escape from the spot.

We hurried with the Indian down the mountain, and on reaching a branch tried to resus-
citate him. Poor fellow! he had gone nearly
too far toward the eternal jungle of game—the
Digger Indian's heaven—to be recalled; but
when at last he opened his gleamy black eye,
and knew he was receiving friendly care, it was
worth much to the heart to see the unmistakable joyfulness that printed its glad image upon
his tawny face. By signs and grimaces he
made us to understand that he was resting at
the tree when, before he knew he was near,
the madman rocked him; that he was rising
to fly when a stone smote him on the temple
and felled him; that he couldn't get away, but
comprehended every thing till, after many
throws, the maniac hit him in the forehead.
He imitated his screams and fantastic leaps,
and conveyed to us, by dismal groans and contortions, the horror he experienced ere he became insensible.

The following afternoon Tom climbed a steep
to kill a deer we had observed to pass that
point several evenings. Becoming impatient,

he pushed on to the crags of Crazy Mountain, as we now called the one a mile east of us; and, killing a deer near its crown, he sought the haunt of the maniac to leave him a portion. Reaching the Indian's tree, he pursued the path till it ended in a clump of hut-like rocks, among which were bones and feathers, but no sign of fire, evidently tokens of the maniac's feast on raw game. Depositing part of his venison there, he had proceeded a third of the distance tentward when he was staggered by a blow from behind, and was furiously grappled by the madman, uttering screams of rage throughout the conflict. It was nearly sundown when we heard mournful calls far up the labyrinth; and Mack exclaimed, "That's Tom, and he is in trouble!"

We ran rapidly till we met him, tottering under the maniac's dangling body. He exclaimed: "I have killed the poor old man! I didn't mean to; wished only to stun him to save myself."

He remained speechless after the few words of explanation, and looked like the statue of grief while we stanched his wounds that were bleeding profusely. As we turned quickly to examine the maniac, he knelt at his head. "Life," I said, as the heart fluttered against my fingers; and tears-gushed from his eyes, and he whispered: "If the mountain were a pearl, I would give it that the old man should live. I smote him only when I thought myself dying in his strangling grip. For a world of crowns I would n't be his slayer."

We hurried with the insensible form to the tent. His struggle with mad death was fearful. Shrieks of rage, howls, fierce efforts to beat us down and escape; feigned quiet, followed by precipitate attacks upon us; eyes of monstrous glare leaping and fastening upon one, then another; sleeplessness, railings of hot hate, were on the third day bound by the soft breath of sleep, whose sprites flooded him with subduing harmonies. For smiles rippled in his furrowed face till it lost its furious glow and wore a tender, cheerful expression; and he said in his slumber: "Play it again, Joli. Nothing, child, is so sweet to me as your voice and harp."

Mack whispered to us: "I thought so. I know him now. 'Joli'—pretty—is what he called his little girl; her brother, 'Phonse;' her mother, 'Verité.' His revolutionary principles forced him from France to New Orleans, where he taught me French. He left there for Cuba."

But we were again listening to the old dreamer on his bear-skin pallet, as he murmured: "The Plaza d'Armas quivers to-night with merry beauties, and the flowers vie with their gems to tint them with witchery; but thou, Joli, art prettiest of the Havandras."

Then he breathed quicker for a little while, and was quiet. But soon we heard him whisper: "Sing it again, child; sing! It was your mother's song—Verité's song. Verité, *my* Verité!"

And heaven gushed in his wrinkled cheeks. Not heaven, but the *love* of long ago, when those cheeks were young and florid, lived again in his gray heart till it forgot that it was old and dreary now, and made his gladdest memory a present reality.

An hour plunged from the sun's face, and the maniac's sleep was too deep to be disturbed by its flight into oblivion, for as it traced its swift course he rested seemingly as rest the dead; and his face grew paler, and the veins grew blue upon his fair old brow; and marble-like repose drew its white, hard sheet over his features; and through their half-opened eyelids his eyes shone glazed and still, and his form moved not. But a glossy feather that had quivered on a quail's crown, when held to his nostrils, veered softly to and fro as if bathing in an infant's breath. So we knew that life yet kinged the struggle, and we watched in hope, moving noiselessly, like dumb children, about the gray misfortune who slumbered in our care.

Then the sun dipped behind a peak and left sunset on its brow, and cast upon the sky vapors of pink; and soft-winged twilight drooped upon the cliffs and ravines, and sung a dreamy lullaby to nature till she fell asleep in dark, who opened her weird bosom to give her rest. And the stars peeped through the dusky pines upon us, and their glances melted in the dim haze; and the air whispered to the old sleeper, and, drawing its ether robes about it, floated on till midnight came, and early dawn; and yet he slept. And sunrise laughed at him from Crazy Mountain, and rolled down upon him floods of glory-beams that piled in purple bubbles over him, and woke him up, and tossed him up on his elbow. He looked earnestly, like an astonished child, at each of us, at his own garb, his hands, the tent, slowly twirled his beard, and rested his wondering eye upon Mack. We held our breath. Some power—perhaps the mysterious flame in his eye — made us know that the passing moment was the crisis with the lost old man, who, sheerly exhausted, fell to the pallet, and whispered: "It's Mack; it can be no one else."

We bathed his hands and face in warm water, and brought him drink from the cold rill hard by that seemed to bubble the merrier as the fainting old maniac, a maniac no longer, slept again.

"He'll die now," said Tom. And his rough face looked beautiful for the womanly tenderness that suffused it and gave to the words the heart-melody that thrills like notes from another, better world. But it was not pale death with the old Frenchman; for he awoke in his right mind, and very much strengthened.

Unhappily his story was the oft-told one. What little reason gambling losses had left him was crazed by "the flowing bowl," till delirium tremens one night hustled him out into the jungle. His son Phonse, who we soon brought to him, had vainly sought him many days, and had given him up as lost forever in some abyss, like many another whose life and dream of wealth together had perished in the gold jungle, when, where, how, none shall ever know. A few days after he and Phonse had begun to mine near us, he came into our pit incapable of speech for a time, but presently said: "You deem me silly, I know, and dread that I am going crazy again. But not so, not so. I have had hideous thoughts like rude dreams of late. Desolate loneliness, dark mountains, doleful abysses; granite clumps like crumbled towers, peopled with horrible forms and sounds; sleeplessness, mad ravings, struggles with fiends, murder, have been rehearsing in my brain. Tell me, boys, where you found me. What doing? How surrounded? Was blood upon my hands? Had I slain any one? Speak *out.* This suspense, this toiling back through memory's wilds of grating forms and voices, will kill me."

And he wept only as the aged weep—not struggling with the grief, nor murmuring that it is, but as if sorrowing most of all that it had fallen upon others. Mack had stepped to his side, and with a woman's intuition that never errs when it seeks to allay the tumults of the heart, replied: "We'll tell you every thing; will go to the places with you. You spent several weeks lost in the mountains before we met you. But be assured that you have killed no one. You did knock an Indian senseless, and would have sent him on the eternal hunt, but when you turned from him to procure more rocks to stone him with, we fled with him to our camp. He left us the next morning happy as a chief, loaded with provisions and old clothing."

His face mantled with delighted relief, but he said, "Well?"

"Well," answered Mack, smiling, "Roth, there, always feels tired when heavy work is to be done, so he left us to pry up bowlders the following afternoon and went hunting up your mountain, for which you knocked him down as an intruder, and were strangling him when he stunned you with a knot, and started here with you. We heard him whooping, and went to his aid. When your brain-fever died out you recognized me, and have made us happy ever since by tarrying here with us. We will go up the mountain with you when you wish and examine the places where you lived."

Luckily a few months dropped into his hand many pounds of gold, and wafted him back to Cuba happy as a Frenchman can well be outside of a revolution. Indeed, it appeared that all he lacked to make him ecstatic was to be in Paris manipulating a jubilee of barricades. His articles of faith were two only:

1. Roman Churchism and monarchy are the bane of France.

2. Republicanism is felicity.

His words of the first were Heclaian slag at white heat. His words of the last were phrased ecstasies.

CHAPTER XII.

PIKE—THAT ECHO REHEARSES WITH A MUSIC
SO STRANGE.

OTH and the brown donkey were
accompanied by another donkey
when they returned from the
nearest store, whither they had
gone fifteen miles, over spurs and
ravines, to make gastronomic discoveries. He
said, as we were discussing the new donkey's
good points: "We shall need both, and many
more, to pack our gold, after awhile, to some
point that wagons can reach."

Mack's eye twinkled at this naïve revelation
of Tom's gold dream, and danced as he observed
the flood of reciprocal humor that washed the
face of the Missourian—a tall, swarthy, frank,
quiet yet sprightly specimen, whom also he had
brought with him, and called Pike. He had
helped him out of a desperate affray with some
"claim-jumpers," near the store, who had
clubbed to kill him, as he would not peaceably
yield most of his mine to them. His wounds

were slight, and he was soon in the placers delving for their hid treasure with us. But they failed to pay in a few weeks, and making no new discoveries we moved many days southward.

Pike left us much to ourselves on the route, for he often diverged to prospect, or hunt, or converse with the scattered miners; but never failed to find our camp of nights. His woodcraft was a marvel, and he convoyed us safely out of many a tangle of thicket and cliff.

Once, about an hour after night-fall, he came to camp and displayed a quartz specimen of singular beauty and richness. The blent blue and white quartz, thickly studded with gold through and through in every part, caused it to sparkle in the fire-light like a clump of compressed stars. It weighed more than a pound. And Pike, as he held it in one and another position, to show its value and varied beauty, said: "If a chap were to send this chunk o' beauty to his sweetheart, would n't it entrance her? An't it a memento? She'd stow it away snug enough in her keepsake drawer, but she'd wrap the chap up in her heart for good and allus.'

I give Pike's words, but not as he would spell or pronounce them. He would spell "memento," for instance, *mi-men-ter*, and so pronounced it. Yet I am sure we will not catch the freshness of his spirit so well on this plan as we would were he admitted to our presence in his own vernacular; for the reason that no translation can give all the phases of the original. His speech put a spell upon Roth deeper and sweeter by far than the specimen had, for his eyes were dewy as if a softest memory had shaped a loving face in them, and he said in a flutter: "Pike, I'll give you three hundred dollars for it, for Leina."

"No," he answered, "can't sell it. A weazel-headed Mississippian gave it to me to-day about ten o'clock. I was telling him who was my partners, and when I said Tom Rothleit, he sprung up out the pit, and looked about wild-like and said flutterously, 'Where in h—l is he?' So you see, Tom, he thinks you belong to the hot place, if you an't there. But I told him you were n't there yet, but were on the way with Mack and Quien somewheres in the jungle, and that it was no use trying to head you off. He give me this yellow rose quartz, and said: 'Give it to Tom for his little girl, and tell him that he saved my life on the Isthmus when my comrades deserted me to die with cholera on the Chagres River.'"

"Aha! it is Skelt," Tom replied; "but he would have got well anyhow."

"Yes," said Pike, "may be so; I do n't know about that. But when he give it to me to bring to you, he said, 'It's nothing to send him, I know;' and his face twitched and he turned his eyes up a tree to keep me from seeing the drops in 'em. And may be so I would have been living too, for all the knives and pistols of them claim-jumpers; but it's mighty fortunate, anyhow, that Tom Rothleit's lively thumps and numb skull was atween me and some of 'em."

Pike's speech had an abrupt turn here, for a grizzly waddled along the side of the spur in pistol-shot of us, and he added hurriedly, "Do n't shoot, do n't shoot!"

The grizzly's dunnish hair looked glossy in the star-light, and though he stood up full breast to us to survey us, he gave token of neither any great surprise nor of any fear nor rage. He appeared like a huge old darky, full of fun, waiting for a company of boys whom he loved, to begin a frolic. We gave him no signal, so he sauntered on over rock and log and spur—hunting, may be, his beloved, who, true to the sex, was leading him a race. When he disappeared, we restored our unused revolvers to their belts, and listened to a narrative from Pike, as follows: "There's game in grizzlies, boys. Do n't provoke 'em 'cept you are safe. Unless you brain 'em, or heart 'em, or shiver their backbones, or unj'int their necks first shot, you are bound to go under. That's why I told you not to shoot just now. If you had n't killed him first fire, thar would have been more skeletons than his left here.

"Old Rackansac pulled trigger with me among the Comanches an' in Mexico. He were a brave one, and as cool and as hot in a scrimmage as Sattan would hev him. He could lay his bullet on a dime, at off-hand a hundred yards, four out o' five times. He got mad arter grizzlies when he come to this country, and was allus a-slopein' through the mountains lookin' up a carouse with 'em. He trimmed the hide off a heap o' 'em too, and sold enough o' their keer_cases to keep him a-going. One Sunday he were a-fixin' his rifle mighty keerful, an' we knew he were for bars that day. We told him to stop it and stay in camp Sundays anyhow, but you might as well have cavorted roun' a hithen. I follered him over the ridge an' tried to decoy him back, for I felt sartin he were wrong, and if he took that hunt it were his last one.

"My mother used to say to me when I were a boy, 'Racket, quit your pranks when Sunday comes. Feed your dog well, an' let him sleep all day. No rabbits of Sundays, Racket, do you hear. Ef you hunt o' Sundays, something bad will come of it.' And all the time I was inducin' old Rackansac to turn back, I seemed to be a-hearin' her blessed voice talkin' it all over to me. But at last he told me to go to—well, som'ers, and he would go a-huntin' ef he went thar, too. An' he went to both of 'em may be, a-huntin' anyhow.

"Night arter night come, and no Rackansac were heered of. But not long arter that, some hunters found a skeleton; a bone here, another thar, a broke rifle, an' close by another skeleton of a big bar with a bowie-knife stuck in the skull. He'd shot that bar through the shoulders, for thar was the bullet-holes, and druv his knife into his brain, for he were game anywhere; but the bar killed him for all that. An' the wolves had gnawed all the meat off them like they had been beasts together. But that bar would never hev got him without help."

"Stuff!" sneered Tom; "you know nobody helped the bear."

"It was n't nobody," he retorted, "it were a misfort'nate providence taking keer of Sunday and leaving its despiser unprotected-like to perish. I hev bad luck, plenty of it; but it come in a honester way than insultin' Sundays to bring it on. Rackansac would hev killed that bar afore he growled, ef it were on his own day. He knew he were wrong, for he told me so just afore he told me to go to—som'ers. It are better to rest on Sunday instid o' trampin' on to it like hithens."

As a rock from the bluff splashed in the branch near us, an alarmed deer bounded past chased by coyotes. We fired into the pack that scattered with affrighted yelps in every direction.

"Them creeters," said Pike, "allus 'mind me of politicians and editurs that puffs whisky, and them that sells it, but howl and snaps at laws and folks anent it. Them and Sattan laps at the same puddles."

"Doubted," interjected Tom; "for Satan do n't use water by drops even."

"Ef you 'd ever noticed," he rejoined, "them that writes up whisky-shops an' them that run 'em, you 'd a known I did n't mean puddles o' water. They look like they 'd sucked brandy-bottles until they was puffed with red Sattans. Free whisky an' free lunch, without water, is their *choice* dishes. A kag o' brandy will buy

7

'em. They put p'ison, *theirn*, on all that's good, an' honors the wust things; like coyotes that fondle wolves, an' gnaw in pieces fawns."

"You will never get to Congress, Pike," replied Tom.

"I am not a-wantin' to," he said. "Editurs make Congressmen, an' the pure editurs can · make too few on 'em. So the wust can'dates goes thar. Old Zack Taylor could n't stand *them;* they smelt him to death in a year, and he were a hard one, seasoned in the Mexican war. It takes lawyers like you to stand Congress; they is *soaked* fur it."

The reports drawn from our revolvers by the coyotes were repeated several times by echo, who threw airily back to us every halloo we uttered, as though the sprites of dell and hill were pelting one another with exhilarating ether from the faces of the cliffs. By this time the coyotes, very like small, trim, light-brown dogs, flanked us, and had gathered on the thicket's border eastward. They were not in position to be echoed, so we escaped a multiplex riot of shrewish howls adapted to evoke imps and set them firing rock and air in a fury of disgust. Our echo would not echo them.

On changing our position a score or more of steps, we were greeted with two other echoes in addition to the first—one of which, far away in the labyrinth, threw back our words to us in tones so musically soft that we closed our ears to every other sound and stood hearkening for its tones as the infant listens for the mother's voice. Mack said, after we resumed our seats: "That echo rehearses with a music so strange that the heart goes out after it as after some sweet hope long lost, throwing back tenderest calls to approach and be blessed. Echo is a word's ghost. The word dies, but repeats itself in echo. Echo is life's ghost. Life hushes in death, but over in the regions beyond repeats itself in echo, and moves on in echo, in purity in the strange land of spirits if it had been pure in the body. For as the sound is here, so is it on yon crag in echo. If it be musical and clear here, it is the same over there in echo, only more so. If it be the reverse here, so is it there in echo."

"I thank you for the thought, Mack," said Roth; "it is tender and chaste like woman. And how many good lives are here that shall exist beyond the boundaries of time, in added tints of glory by God's hand, to adapt them best for residence in heaven but should be echoed in other lives here! Once upon the sea, in a palace-steamer eight or ten days from port, we saw, at the setting in of darkness, far away directly in front of the ship's prow, a lurid star rise out of the billows and dip back, rise and re-dip for many minutes, growing larger and larger each bath. Then it shone steadily just above the billows, enlarging, dropping into the sea, springing up again, quivering, nodding, staring, flaming, brighter and larger meeting us. We climbed upon chairs and benches and rope-coils, and into the cordage of the mysterious masts throwing their arms about wildly above us; and all eyes were bent upon the witching wonder walking the dark waves. It nestled on them, oscillated, expanded, rolling toward us, looking in the darkness like some magic wonder riding the sea.

"Presently one whispered, 'A burning ship!' and the words moaned from heart to heart till the agony voiced them in a shout of many voices, 'A burning ship! a burning ship!' Then, dumbed by the horror, still we watched. Soon the thunder of its machinery and laboring furnaces and the crash of its frantic wheels were heard in the thick night, and wild, brave calls from its signaling whistle shouted athwart the dark and the deep. Still right onward it rushed, and right onward we plunged to it. Now we had so nearly approached that the star had severed into many great fragments, pouring shine out of and about the brilliantly lighted ship, from as many rifts in its white sides and glowing roof, till itself and objects on its galleries, the men, women and children peopling its decks, were visible to us. And these were observing us as eagerly and as safely as we were beholding them. And all the way, thirty-six hundred miles, and all the time—day, night—that and this had been bounding, on the wings of steam and storm, over an ocean air-line, rushing together; when, as we thought, 'They will surely crash into each other and sink together here,' this veered to the west, that to the east. Each tossed rockets into the night's cloud, and their masters trumpeted messages to each other as they passed, and the passengers cheered across the yawned wave. Then each veered into the watery air-line again, and away, away over mountain and chasm of sea, each strained to its destined port, bearing its life-freight safe to shore at last. Each seemed an echo of the other.

"To me, the incident was a reminder of pure characters on the sea of life—each to trust true, neither in another's way, though the same path pursuing; voyaging this way and that, increasing knowledge, hopefully signaling each other on the throbbing billows."

"It is a joy to look upon such characters," said Mack, "to hear the flutter of their sails, to see the plunge of their prows, the dip and plunge and roll, their onward push, the stretch and swell of their taut cordage, the glint of their portly sides—for all within is peace and good-will to God and man. They are floating havens, illuminated and furnished to save the wrecked on the main, to brave the tempestuous breakers till the tossed voyagers are safely tided to the quiet shore.

"Such men, such women are shower and sunshine to the world. They invest wastes with verdure, make the desert heart to blossom as the rose. They bind up, build up, pacificate. Everywhere—some greater, some less—upon life's seditious floods they sail. In fog, in clear, in belt of calms, in belt of storms, off on the trade-wind currents, fanned by the breeze, rocked by the hurricane, each in place struggling forward, drifting life-boats after the lost, availing all means for the ministry of happiness, dispensing life and light in storm and quiet till they shall knock at the eternal docks, course finished, sails furled, steam off, wheels at rest, the 'Good Master' aboard inspecting, saying, 'Well done.' *This* world were happier echoing their pure principles."

In the lull of conversation now, we were startled by the grating rattle of a serpent that struck over the spot whence we had leaped at the warning. It coiled in a moment again, its tremulous rattle whizzing in its ire; but Pike's revolver flashed bullets through its spotted folds, and it stretched itself out and died; and Pike said: "Tom, I heerd you say onct, in one of your tantrums, that 'demagogues in Church and State, like them that tarries long at the wine, was rancid moralities, cancerous intellectuals, poisonous serpents, effluviating the sea of humanity; an' that the wise should keep apart from them.' This spotted fellow is one of their sort, and I will drag him to the coyotes at the thicket. Them snappy, snarly howlers will soon put him out o' sight, more 'n you are likely to do with your 'demagogues in Church and State,' as you call 'em. Thar's too many to echo them brazen, imperdent, piznous kerakters. An' nothin' ekels 'em on arth in 'front'ry, 'cept your 'maginary tons o' gold."

CHAPTER XIII.

PHANTOM OR NO PHANTOM, HE SHALL NOT DIE
IN THE COLD.

HE gold phantom beguiled us into unfrequented placers, in a region so rugged that even Indian trails had disappeared, and busied us in collecting their nuggets of gold, which, whatever their virgin purity, were small and scarce as tears of joy. Yet we noted little else. Even November was passing freezingly away, and still gold's song, from among the ice-coated rocks, made us heedless of the thickening mists marshaling among the heights, videttes of the storm, rising out of the sea to break in sleet and snow upon the dwellers among the peaks.

The maniac tempest now rolled over us, banking the snow - clouds upon the cliffs where, breaking in pieces, they leaped into the placers like sheeted thunders, and congealed in white waves upon every thing; and in a few days the jungle of mountains appeared like a stranded

snow-world, upon which icy blasts incessantly
poured foaming breakers that froze to it as if
to sink it in a sea of ice. We took the alarm
at last, and struck out in the tempest in quest
of a softer clime. We had tramped two days
through the sleety wilderness, and, bewildered
by the blasts, had turned again and again upon
our trail in the sunless, tempestuous days.
Mack had sprained his foot by an evil slip upon
the ice, and Pike had tumbled into a gorge,
and sunk to his shoulders in the snow-drift
at its bottom, bruised and stunned by the fall.
And we had just entered a vista winding along
precipices and dismal cañons when he fell
again, tripped by a little snowy hillock; and
puffing the snow from his lips, he exclaimed,
" It are a dead man frized by himself, sartinly!
Unkiver him, boys, unkiver him quick!"

On opening the mound we found the pale
sleeper yet with life; and we rubbed him
roughly, no doubt, but with kindly intent, till
his breathing was healthful; and wrapping
blankets round him, we kindled a fire and
camped for the night. The snow-man seemed
quite restored in an hour or two, and told us
that he had wandered from a hunting party
escaping out of the mountains. In the intervals of the storm he walked along the crest of

the ridge and peered into the gulches as if watching for the coming of some one or essaying to settle the question of our whereabouts —restless, though we strove to make him at ease with us.

The night was black, but the winds were at rest for awhile; and though the snow fell thicker, our brave fire shot red sparkles among its white flakes as though cheering night trying to soothe the sobbing storm upon her bosom. We had improvised a brush tent, whose twigs in their robes of sleet looked like jets of shimmering glass, and we had closely grouped upon our blanketed- ice-couch; and all was hush save the soft patter of the snow-flakes falling into bed upon bough and rock. Erebus himself seemed satisfied with the rare gloom of our situation, when a quick shriek, like that of sudden death, shivered through the icicles over our heads and echoed from glen to glen. We sprung to our feet, but stood motionless. Earth's dead seemed to be tramping lightly, running to and fro around us. Each snow-robed shrub appeared in the moment to be a sheeted ghost started from its grave by the horror, and the dark full of sorrowful whispers.

A glance revealing to me that Roth and

Snow-man were gone, I ventured into the eddying dark, where the flash and report of a pistol guided me toward the place of the scream. Snow-man was expostulating with Roth and an angry Mexican, who lay grappled on the snow too fiercely to use their weapons again. We separated them, and as they rose up Tom said: "I do n't believe a word of it. It was not a tiger's scream; it was a human voice."

"No," replied Snow-man; "I know the Mexican, I tell you; believe him."

Finding that neither was hurt, we moved to the fire, where the Mexican stated that, trying to pierce the mountains to where a few comrades awaited him to move southward, he was nearing our camp when some animal bounded upon him with a scream, but, missing its mark, sped on down the spur; and as he rushed for the fire Tom met him, denied his explanation, and the fight ensued.

"Never mind it, Señor," said Roth pleasantly; "you are cold and hungry. I am glad the ball missed you. Draw nearer the fire. Here is a pan of venison and bread; welcome; help yourself."

He ate eagerly, and in a short while appeared to sleep soundly by Snow-man. It seemed but a few minutes after that I was roused silently, and beckoned aside by Tom, who said, "I have found him."

"Found who?" I queried, vexed at being waked from a much-needed sleep and led out into the whizzing snow.

"Why, the man who shrieked," he whispered. "He's coiled up at the foot of the precipice down yonder—crazy, I guess—nearly dead."

"Tom," said I, "you are forever at some folly. Have you been groping about in this storm and darkness, where one can scarcely be secure by day, hunting a phantom of your own frenzied brain?"

"Yes, I have," he retorted; "and if you won't help me bring him to the fire—as Pike and Mack are both lame—I'll *drag* him here. Phantom or no phantom, he shall not die in the cold."

I have thought since that even at that time it had become a mental habit of mine to question Roth's sanity without being conscious of it. His conduct on occasions was so apart from the customary channels of human nature that are cramped and selfish, seldom filling up and flooding over with prompt, free, fresh, brave concern for the unfriended totterers along life's way, that at least he was

unique to me; and though he controlled me
usually, I imagined it was strength humoring
weakness.   So I skirred out into the icy chaparral with him; and, aided to pick our way
among the bent sleet-clad underbrush by the
snowy sheet that earth had drawn over her
bosom, we soon came to the senseless man, and
bore him up to the camp.   In our absence the
Mexican and Snow-man had vanished.

The wound upon the victim's head, inflicted
by his fall over the bluff, caused his insensi-
bility; for that in his side, betraying the Mexican's knife, was upon a rib.   The knife had
passed through a girdle of gold and glanced,
so the gash next his heart barely sundered the
skin.   Only the depth of snow where he fell
saved his life.   His slumbers were fitful, and
he murmured as he slept of the treachery of
his comrade.   We tended him anxiously till
smiles from the fountain of dreams bubbled
in his face; and the words he muttered were
of home and boyhood and dear faces.   The
hope in his voice, the life and quiet of his
smiles, carried us back across the continent
through the moaning tempest to childhood's
scenes of peace and safety.   And the melodies
of the hearth and play-ground, that were in
the early barbaric days of the gold-fields dews

to the fevered miners, were crisply sung by us; and their notes seemed to impart to those of the fitful tempest a prankish dash that divested it of gloom and filled it with fun. We alternated in keeping guard and sleeping—sleeping mostly; for when the camp was astir in the morning we discovered that Roth and the wounded man were gone. Pike thought they were in pursuit of the Mexican, and said: "Tom's saft - headed, specially about other folks's wrongs. He'd as lief foller Sattan himself ontil they's rectified. He's right ontil his heart saftens like a gal's; then he's onreasonable-like, and will do that way that's got the least sense in it. He's toled the man off arter them chaps, and like as not the Mexican's knife are in his ungumpsious heart afore now Ef he's not dead, he are arter something cleverish, though; and,' he added after a moment's reverie, "ef thar's any chance to make trouble of it, he'll do it, and be in the middle of it himself, like the nateral he are. He might er took me along to help him out on it."

"Perhaps," I suggested, "the man became crazed while we slept and wandered away, and Roth is trying to beguile him into camp again."

"Like as not," he answered, "like as not: for it's like him a-wanderin' over these snow-quags in the marssyless storm arter a frenzied man with a insane sperit. The man will naterally run into the wust places, and he'll follow him or die, and palaver with him everywhere he goes. He'll outfool the fool, and break both o' their necks."

Pike was active as a catamount, though he appeared gangling and clumsy. He never flinched in danger, though at times he seemed fearful; for occasionally he would laugh off serious provocations or be silent, till, not reading him rightly, parties presumed too far, and were surprised by fierce frays, in which he was certain to manipulate victories. His attachment to Roth was ardent, and the more so for the very traits he was now decrying. We immediately followed on the nearly effaced tracks of Rothleit and the wounded man through the thickening tempest till they diverged, and, leaving the stranger's foot-prints to me, Pike pursued Tom's. I traced the white tracks zigzagging from bluff to bluff till it led to the scene of the Mexican's treachery. Here I saw the man looking about in the ravine below, and, attracting his attention, he looked to me and said: "I have given you more trouble; sorry

you came after me.   I was seeking the spot of
last night's peril.   This is it.   I must have
fallen from the bluff to your right, for I found
my pack lodged in the brush at its base.   Nothing lost.   It has twenty pounds of gold in it
besides my blankets.   I 'll meet you round the
angle."

As we sauntered to the camp he told me he
had left Roth asleep, he supposed, and said:
"I am going to ——, to meet my partner; am
a Virginian; been lost in the mountains two
days.   In my wilderment every vista in the
jungle seemed a trail.   Several times each day
I crossed my own tracks; and the first time I
did so I pursued them hastily, and shouted to
the man ahead of me, as I supposed, from
time to time before discovering the mistake.
I came upon the Mexican intent to cross a tor-
rent.   He politely replied to my inquiries, and
proposed, as I was far astray, to pilot me to
his friends' camp to spend the night, whence
I could proceed safely and without difficulty.
On nearing your camp, after worrying in the
darkness through tangles of spurs and chap-
arrals some hours, he said it was the camp we
were seeking.   But he seemed to be restive
and paused—proceeded, paused.   I cannot account for it, but I felt in the moment an al-

most tangible horror seize me—a sense of murder's presence; its red corpse with stretched-open eyes seemed to glare at me, and in the moment his thuggee-stab staggered me, and I knew I was falling from the precipice, when sensibility fled. The next things I remember are a sharp pain and a feeling of being wrapped in a blanket, and the words: '*There*, an't you more comfortable *so?* I am Tom Rothleit. I'll stick to you like a brother. You shall be at the fire presently.' I could not speak, could not move; but I recalled every thing. My heart gave a bound of strange joy, a tender hand glided over my wounds, my brain reeled, whirled, whirled and I was insensible again. The rest you know. But is not the Mexican's conduct unaccountable? If robbery was his object, why did he delay till we neared the fire? If murder only, his opportunities were many, and where human intervention was impossible."

As the day wore away, he and Mack tested their strength by climbing up the mountain two hundred feet or so to a bench from whose points, in intervals of the snow-fall, they could behold the wonders the frost had painted on crags and peaks and forests near and distant. It was an hour to night when Pike returned with a fine deer. He replied to

8

my query concerning Roth by saying: "The ornery wretch is all right, except he's been beside himself more'n ever all the time; an' he are nearly frized and starved. He seed Mack and the stranger upon the side o' the mountain, and he are gone thar to lead 'em into another fool scrape, as he has me to-day. I've limped nigh on to fifteen mile, for'ards and back'ards, a-huntin' him in this hurricane to fetch him in. He were goin' right from camp when I spied him; and he stands to it that he were a-goin' right all the time. He were the wust lost man you ever seen. When I showed him the camp smoke he stuck to it, it were a ice-spout and nothin' else, till he saw the man up thar on the bench on the mountain with his head bound up. He carcumvented him this morning ontil he seen he were n't *abberated,* he called it; and then went to hunt Snow-man and the Mexican. But here they come now."

"Who?" said I, jumping up; "Snow-man and the Mexican?"

"No, you wood-head!" he snapped out; "but Tom and t'others. He says when the uncommonest fool were made, I were the specimen turned out; that you would hev been but for the reason nothin' can't be made out o' nothin'."

CHAPTER XIV.

HE'S FOLLERIN' SATTAN.

IN a day or two we journeyed from "Tempest Camp," as we had named the place, and at noon lunched standing, using the donkeys for tables, the waltzing snowflakes giving the air of sprightliness and neatness to board and contents. Having, California-like, christened the wounded man Virginia, the name of the State he hailed from, Pike, munching a bit of frozen venison, said: "Virginy, ef Mexico had 'ave plunged his knife, the last blow, a inch or two nearer his aim, you couldn't 'ave been here a-eatin' deer-steak off of donkeys. You'd 'ave been under a big snowdrift friz harder nor a icicle."

Happy smiles suffused his face at Pike's cool recall of the perils he had survived, but his reply startled the group, not because Providence was habitually sneered at in the gold-fields—for the reverse is true—but by reason of the reverence and intensity of faith and feeling his simple reply conveyed, as he said: "Yes, but

Mexico's knife in the snows of the Sierras was foiled by a father's whispers in the far-away mists of Chesapeake Bay, speaking my name in the ear of God."

"It were curious whispers," Pike replied, "that turned aside that Mexican's knife. His sort are true to Sattan, and together murder is almost easier to them than mercy is to God. There are many clever Mexicans, but he were n't one."

"Only soul-whispers," he said, "that God answered by the angel that dropped me off the precipice from the stab of Mexico that grazed next the heart."

"But it looks to me," rejoined Pike, "ef a angel had interfered atwixt you and Mexico, he'd a-drapped *him* instead o' you over the bluff and friz him thar 'tarnally. I believe, though, that prayers brings heavenly folk to keep arthly ones safe sometimes. Esau were injured by Jacob, but Jacob prayed and the angels of God met him afore Esau did, and saftened Esau's heart to forgive, till he ran an' kissed Jacob. I have allus sided with Esau in that family trouble. The bold, poor, keerless, bighearted fool Tom, thar, is just like him."

"Some teach," I interposed, "that Bible statements of angelic rescues are as preposterous, as charming, as replete with chimera as with beauty, and should be eliminated from the faith of man."

"Such counsel should have no following," said Virginia. "In its last analysis it is only brassy brilliance. And he who teaches it would rid his race of a pestilence, were he to enact Ahithophel in a Bible statement suggested by these donkey tables; it reads: 'When Ahithophel saw that his counsel was not followed, he saddled his ass, and arose, and gat him home to his house, to his city, and put his household in order, and hanged himself, and died, and was buried in the sepulcher of his father.'"

"And," suggested Tom, "it was not the skeptic literati, whose effrontery scarcely equals their absurdities and shallowness, who said to the king, 'My God hath sent his angel, and hath shut the lions' mouths, that they have not hurt me,' but Daniel, 'skillful in all wisdom, *understanding* science, and kneeled upon his knees three times a day, and prayed before his God.' And, Quien, with the doubts you rehearse, you may as well take Virginia at his word, go like Ahithophel and die, and be buried in the sepulcher of your father; it will be warmer than this snow-storm."

"Tom," interposed Pike, "you are flutter-

somer of words nor a flutter-mill are o' water-
draps.   Why did n't you tell him at onct, and be
done with it, that the Scriptur says thusly and
so; an' ef he 's no sensibler than to believe rock-
head sciencers afore Scriptur, he 's follerin'
Sattan and agoin' to him.   That 's your mean-
in', the whole on it."

CHAPTER XV.

SNOW-BALLING WITH SNOW-CLOUDS.

HE next day's slow course filled us with dismay. Alp-like groups environed us. We were going into instead of out of the Sierras. The clouds, like moving ice-worlds, grated and fretted over us. Stalactic icicles fell in fragments along our frigid way, or depended from the saplings to the snow-beds. The iced firs and pines, whose foliages of prismy leaves, like snow-blossoms, were ever whispering the tempest, dropped their pearly petals upon us. The clumpy thickets, each twig a crystal, limbs interlocked, holding specimen brilliants of varied shapes molded by the genius of the frost, made the waste look like a "World's Fair" of fine glass—each tiny and larger vessel ringing melodies at pleasure of Æolus; while creation—bathing, ever bathing in the snow-floods, throwing upon every thing shrouds woven by the spirits of the storm—waited above, beneath, about us, till we felt like muffled sighs tossed from blast to blast.

We were lost in the wild of ice, floundering in the Sierras' sea of snow. Pike stood upon his head "to git the right bearin's," he said; Virginia whistled "Yankee Doodle;" Tom followed Mack and me from shrub to shrub as we chopped tender branches and frailed the sleet off for the donkey's forage, and charged us to embalm and send him home to Leina; "for," he said, "she would n't like for me to be buried in any such a devilish country as this."

Just then we were arrested by Pike's shrill whistle, and looking in the direction he pointed we beheld a splendid buck bounding across the plateau; and, as he passed a thicket, a grizzly darkened his pale path, quick as a twinkle, and slew him in mid-air. Between foot-lift and footfall glowy with life, rigid in death, bruin sprung to his victim and placed his paw upon him, then bent over and took his neck between his jaws and crunched it, and reared upon his haunches and leered at us.

"He 's a Sattan!" exclaimed Pike; "come, we 'll speak to him with rifles 'bout that trick."

As we approached, the bear started into the thicket, but dashed suddenly back with a fierce growl, bounding upon us amid pelting bullets, and was in less than twenty paces of us when Pike's rifle was leveled and fired, apparently in

the same moment, and he tossed back—a quivering mass—for the bullet had crashed through
his brain.

"That shot saved us," said Mack, "for not
another pierced him. I shot for the heart."

"And you did n't miss it fur," said Pike as
he pointed to a little red spot; "that draps from
mighty near your mark. A old Texas-ranger,
though, do n't often make as bad a shot as that,
Mack. You an't in practice of late. Shot 'mos'
too quick. An Injun would a-got you, ef your
pistol had n't a-follered up your rifle quick, and
truer o' aim."

Taking from him his robe of fur to sleep upon,
and a few pounds of steak, we left the carcass
with the greater part of the deer, and a half-
mile farther on camped in an angle of huge
rocks. Shortly after dark the howl of hoarse-
mouthed wolves, mixing with the shriller voices
of the tempest, assured us that bruin and his
buck were soon to be no more, even in carcass.
Several crept across the fire-line watching us
with glarry eyes, whose glances we answered
by bullets to the death of one of the band. He
fell when about to attain his wolfy ambition,
a fat carcass; like man halted by death's bolt
in the very glitter of the carcanet he rejects
heaven for, but is never to wear. Indeed, we

were all near concluding that we would exchange all the linked wonders of gold to be out of the congealed wonders of nature, that froze us in on every side.

At times through the night the tempest soughing through the jungle, growling round the crags, was appalling. Every now and then a monster crash wailed in the darkness as a peak shook from his brow a midnight avalanche; while occasionally the awful rush and roar were several times repeated in quick succession, as though the gods dethroned in Olympus had refuged here and were snow-balling one another with snow-clouds. Amid their lumbering carousal, Pike said: "Ef we jest had a par o' compasses, we'd skeet out o' this muss like monkeys out o' cocoa-nut-trees. Them ar little things is smart as Roth *thinks* he are. They says nothin' and pilots right; he's 'tarnally directin' and allus wrong."

Before Tom, in his low-spirited condition, could reply, Virginia took from the cover of a small book a jewel not larger than a thumb-nail, and placed it in Pike's hand, having in the wilderment of all the tempestuous days forgotten it. Pike held it in his leveled palm and its diminutive needle dipped, whirled, trembled, then stood quivering, pointing due north.

"Hooray! hooray!" exclaimed Pike. "Whar *did* you git it?"

"Two years ago," replied Virginia, "when I was starting to the gold-fields—a blue-eyed Kentucky lass gave me the Testament with the golden compass in its clasp."

"And you an't read it neither," said Pike; "it's bright as the compasses."

"O yes I have, but with washed hands," replied Virginia; "read it again and again."

"But with washed hands!" said Pike; "that's as much as to say to me, 'Don't you tech the book until you run a bushel o' snow through your smoked hands.'"

"Not a word of it," he said pleasantly; "*there.*"

Pike took the book, handling it tenderly as though he thought it to be a flower from heaven, turned a few pages, and exclaimed: "Waal! an't she a critter for beauty? What's you a-sayin', Mum?"

And she was beautiful—that blonde Kentuckian whose picture he had found between the book's pure pages; and sheltering it from the snow-flakes he scanned, by the fire-light, her sun-print, with the clear eye of as gentle and brave a heart as ever flashed admiration.

We were all happier after beholding the serene shadow. She noted not the storm nor heeded the gods carousing among the crags; but looked quietly, cheerily, trustingly into our eyes amid the flutter of the tempest and the riftless gloom of the dark night.   On her right a vase of japonicas, roses, and lilies stood; and in her lap a bunch of smaller flowers nestled in green leaflets.   Her left-hand rested upon an open book, her right clasped a locket; and from her neck a medallion drooped on her bosom.   She said nothing, yet there were the fresh lips that had spoken words of love, sung many pure sentiments, and said, "Our Father who art in heaven."   There were her eyes that had showered many smiles, and possibly many tears—for even gentle woman weeps this side heaven.   I never saw it so that I did not feel that sin is an ungallant monster.

That which makes woman weep other than tears of joy, or sympathy, or saintly penitence, is an unmitigated shape of evil; and he who occasions it is a wretch, though purpled with power and fame and worldly pleasures, and honored by her love.   She is God's smile upon the path of man.   However fallen, *however* fallen, the germ of the angel lies budding in her heart. And when robed in knowledge and innocence, her presence is a charm that attaches man to the heavenly and the true.

CHAPTER XVI.

THAT LION WERE A GIRL-LION.

I̅ was an hour to day-break ere we were out of our frosty bed. The storm had taken on a darker hue; the snow was harder, rounder, like white shot. We had given our faces a snow-bath, and were turning one cheek to the fire, then the other, when Pike, quietly catching up his rifle, stepped between the blaze and some object, trying to catch an aim on it. Again and again he tried, while we were intently peering into the darkness. Presently we beheld the fierce, beautiful glare of eyes flashing full upon us a moment like fiery stars, then disappearing, now appearing, now gone out; and for a minute's space the startling specters went and came, when the crack of the rifle started us from almost under our scalps. There were a few leaps toward us, and within the fire-circle the writhing form of the California lioness rolled upon the ice floor, and bounded back into the darkness as the ready volley of pistols echoed in the jungle.

We listened to the irregular bounds of the lithe creature speeding into the thick night till its crash upon the snow could be heard no more. Pike turned to the fire, and said: "I've killed many deer at night by shining their eyes; but that brownish varmint shot red coals out o' hers at me too onconstant for me to draw a bead atween 'em; so she's 'scaped. She were arter the donkeys, but Tom's prettiness aside of them struck her all aheap, and while she were a'mirin' of him I saluted her. She are a gal, you may be sure; for they is allus a-pryin' into things, a-gettin' into mischief. They's been curious ever sence and afore one on 'em bit a apple. Ef I were married to one o' them consarns, I'd keep her allus mighty loving. I'd let on that I knowed somewhat that oughtn't to be told nohow to nobody, and she'd honey me to crack o' doom a-hopin' to fuddle it from me. I tell you, boys, that lion were a gal; for nothin' but gal curiosity could 'ave drawed her out her cave in sich a storm. They's allus bent on goin' where and when they oughtn't to, I've heern tell. She'd better been in her pa's parler among the rocks; or ef she's married, she'd much better been brushin' her husband's furry coat and whiskers at home. But that's the last thing

they ever is, satisfied to stay at home. They soon
curious through home things, an' must prance
round in their pretty gear to see ef all the
fools is married yet, or to see the sights, an'
diskiver the secrets of their own kind. Wonder they do n't run theirselves off their insteps
a-curiousing into things. But one thing are
sartin, they's the beautifulest thing in natur.
That lion's eyes an't a carcumstance o' splendor aside of theirs. And arter all, they's the
best things in natur. Their voice is music,
their tech is life. I were wounded once in
Mexico, and one o' them black-eyed Mexican
critters brought me the things I'd axed for,
but I did n't have sense enough to know I want-
ed 'em. She were cream-colored, except each
cheek were a pink. She had orange-blossoms
in her black hair, and allus carried a han'ful o'
boquays. She'd be round a dozen on us at a
time. A kind word, a smile, a bright flower,
a saft tech, a sasserful o' just the things we
needed, an' away she tripped, like the innercent she were, to make another squad feel better and think better of her race. Arter that,
ef I sighted a Mexican in battle, and he were
at all like her, I'd shoot somebody else; for
her eyes would 'pear to be thar a-sayin', 'That's
my brother,' or 'That's my sweet'art;' and I

couldn't a-shot 'em ef old Zack Taylor had been thar sayin', 'Shoot 'em, Racket; shoot 'em!' But that's neither here nor thar. That lion were a girl-lion, curiousing around in her brown furs, a-seein' what she could see."

"Missing your lionly mark, Pike," said Virginia, "makes you piquant. Curiosity, unless it pries and is unkind, discounts neither the lioness nor one of those black-eyed Mexican creatures with hair full of orange-blossoms. Polished, reticent, chaste, it is a grace that should note and report only charming discoveries."

"It should be the humming-bird," suggested Mack, "observing the sweets and beauties of each flower, fluttering soft music, pausing on tremulous wing to chirp a song of the elixirs—not the poisons—it uncaps. Here, there, everywhere, touching every thing gracefully that is sweet and beautiful, this fairy of the flower-yard is delightedly welcomed by the old and the young. Each is quiet lest the tiny grace miss a blossom or chirp a note less ere it disappears to wake May-day in other hearts, humming none but cheery stories of the sad and glad flowers it had shimmered before. Voyaging from sweet scene to sweet scene only, it darts around or skips over from sight of all that is not fragrant, lest its nice ear should catch a harsh sound, or its sensitive eye be smitten by a blightful color, or its chaste wing be burdened by an ill, or its flossy bosom be ruffled by a rude breath, and its dainty tongue give an evil and not a kindly note."

"When it's that way," rejoined Pike, "it are good and right. But more'n like that—I mean too of'n—it are like a sarpent trailing through the flower-gardens of serciety breaking down and pizining the sweetest blooms. And womankind an't got the most on it neither. Lestways I 've seen a heap o' men as spouts it, as like enough they might be sea-sarpents in that line. They's to be targets for Indian arrows at short range, wus nor the lion a-tryin' to make even a innercent donkey a prey."

9

CHAPTER XVII.

IN A TANGLE OF DREAMS—I MUST SEE THAT RIVER OF STONE.

UIDED by the little compass, we turned westward. Depth nor height nor tempest veered its bright point from its polaric mark; for like woman's heart, however it throbbed and vibrated at the tumult, as if repulsion to evil inhered, it was defiantly true to its invisible love.

At times the dervishes of the storm tripped us from our footing as they leaped by, decorating our path with white garlands; or the snow-queen threw her foamy veil over us in folds thick enough to blind us. But at night we halted in a group of tough oaks, and banking the snow around us four or five feet high, we collected logs and limbs for an all-night fire. About midnight the roar of the tempest ceased, the winds were at rest. The jungle was noiseless as Tyre's forest of marble columns dreaming in the pale sea, except at long intervals a sleet-clad pine unbound his snow-

crown, and shattered it upon the white forum.
In the mystic calm our senses were keen yet
soothed. The quivering din of the storm was
replaced by the silent flow of lethe flooding its
wake, and bathing us in a freshet of soft sensations. Yet the snow fell, but so quietly we
knew it not by sound, and in the hush the wilderness, like a nearly drowned Triton escaped
to shore, breathed sighs of relief, till the stars
flooded the cleared heavens and the icy earth
with brightness. Our hearts became as quiet
as nature's sleep, amid the softness and beauty
of the downflow of the star-flood; and we
stepped without the circle of the fire-light to
drink in the scene's witchery. The thousands
of icicles were like crystal prisms bathing in
and reflecting pale flames, and the tree-boughs
and all shrubs drooping with ice momentarily
imprisoned and loosed from their shimmery
caresses the sky rays, till every thing seemed
arrayed in diamonds of changeful glamours.

I unconsciously moved on till a ridge was
placed between me and the camp, and was beholding the pale waste, and listening to the
music the zephyrs, like invisible bell-ringers,
were ringing from the silvery ice-bells, when
an unearthly "Halloo-o-oo!" startled me, till I
rolled pell-mell down the hill, loosening as I

went hundreds of shattered icicles, scaling, ringing, clattering into the frozen gorge. I picked myself up industriously, however, and answered the call. A hatless German at once advanced to me. A blanket, through whose center he had thrust his bald head, dropped in frozen folds about his fat form, and he said: "Lose mein way. No stopt; no preat, no lager, no schmoke, no nudding, but stirm since yester morn; find plenty wulfs, pite preeches-leg, pite hat; coldt hedt, foot, potty, all over; whew! Peen mining one fool gulch, no golt; want lager, start to trade-post, snow thick, wind blowt hedt all wrong, no know nudding, go all 'pouts, wulfs roat, pite at me up tree, runs me pout veer meucht, gits hadt; whew!"

Pike's face twitched with humor as the German repeated his story at the camp; but as he was appeasing his hunger with coffee and deer and bread, Pike said: "When the troops were marchin' atween Saltillo and Jalapa in the Mexican scrimmage, I fell out of ranks with the army cramps, that was cholery or something as bad, and the ambulance missed me. That night as I lay alone expectin' to die with the stars awinkin' and laughin' at me, a Dutchman lifted my head and put his coat under me, and kivered me with his blanket, and poured a mixter down my throat that wern't hard to swallow; an' next day got me to a safe place. He were chubby, an' his head were bound up like Virginy's, for a Mexican lance had gashed it, and the hithen creeturs were scrougin' through the country in bands. I told him to *ramose*, or some o' the Sattans would ketch him ef he staid by me that night, and drift a spear into his saft heart. He said: 'Dat nudding, I stickts der you; I *safes* you, den I runs midt all mein foots.'"

"Yah, Racket," said the German, who had recognized him by the story; "I no runs dat nighdt, safes mein foots to run dis nighdt from dere wulfs dat pites de preeches veer meucht up dere tree."

"Well, Heinrich," Pike replied, "you are about the welcomest lost man that ever got to a friend's camp. Ef it wern't for your coming we might believe we was in the valley o' death among the mountains where the silence deepens on a mortal till he comes to a dead halt."

"Dat one forebode," answered Heinrich, "dat never git into mein hedt. Dis no dedt valley. It one flower vorld. De trees, dey flowers of ice. Dere twigs, dere pig and schmal limbs, pe nudding but white flowers, like pig white clumps of flossy feathers. De shrubs pe ice-blossoms dat sing if you touch 'em; and de snow pes sky-flowers clipped off de clouds, singing troe de air coming to de vorld to dress it mit white raiments. No dedt valley; one flower vorld."

"That," said Mack, "is at least Germanic. Your tribe not only fight well, but invest every thing with music and flowers."

"And lager," added Pike.

"And literature," said Tom.

"And labor," said Virginia.

"An' safes der foots der run from de wulfs, wid der preeches-leg pite ofl in de stirm," answered Heinrich, looking at his tattered trousers.

Heinrich was scarcely thawed and warmed ere the south-west blast was again soughing through the rugged congelations, piling dark clouds over us, pushing them against the crags, hurling them through the clefts in the mountains, grinding them together, till in fretted helplessness, dissolving in the elemental strife, they snowed, as Pike said, "thicker an' faster nor I ever see afore."

Virginia, the while, was in a tangle of dreams it seemed; for though his eyes were open and bright, his lips were scaled, and he replied to queries even by signs instead of sounds.

Pike, trying to shell him out, said: "Virginy 'minds me to-night o' a Cherokee human we called River Dick. He mined, or rather 'bibed, nigh onto a river of rock not fur from Sinora. He'd watched fur a stranger to be a-comin' by, an' meet him outside o' the crowd, an' say sorrowfuller nor death: 'I–I–aré near–lee starved; had nuthin' fur gwine on three days; see h–how my v–voice trembles an' han's shakes; can't scacely talk, s–so weak. L–le–let me hev a ha–half d–dollar ter git so–some cheese an' b–b–bread afore death c–c–comes, plase.'"

"In course he got the money, an' he'd go to whar the bread an' cheese was, but allus 'vested the funds in whisky; an' then be a dyin' the same way ag'in. Virginy is solemner nor River Dick a-dyin' arter grog."

Virginia's dream being too sad or too sweet to yield to Pike's grenade, Mack said: "That river of stone is one of the gold-field wonders. I was skirring up a picturesque gorge north of it when I first beheld it. From the head of the gorge to its top is more than a hundred feet. Its sides are perpendicular for much of its outcrop at that point; its surface level, except conglomerate bowlders, some sealed to the surface as if melted to it, lay about like huddles of black cattle sleeping on its bosom. It is over three hundred feet broad. It is a river of rock without banks, whose stone current, swirled bluffy up, flows on noiselessly toward the great plains that bank the San Joaquin tules. On its south side a beautiful little plain rolls against it twenty or thirty feet below its brink. Its walls and surface and windings and scoria suggest that in a fused state it had run down the channel of a river, burying its waters, or tossing them into another bed, by its red floods cooling there. It appears that the hills had been pulled away from it by the hands of many centuries; or the throb of an earthquake had heaved the huge serpentine mass up above surroundings, and left it so, to attest its awful power, whose throes tumble mountains, or raise them, grind the rolling plains and fill the earth with quaking till its populations die amid falling groves and columns."

The description was lost upon Tom at least, except to suggest to him one thought. For he exclaimed: "There lies our pile! A tunnel drifted under the foundations of that river of stone will bring us into the gold deposits accumulated by ages; or, likely, uncap to us the original smithy where the precious metal was first made on this coast; and we shall have to charter the line of steam-ships to convey our tons of gold home."

His early-day phantasy possessed him with wild visions, and made him a tony again. His eyes and voice quivered with delight, and his face was wrapped in ecstasy. I should have regretted Mack's matter-of-fact way, had it not been plain that Tom was too bewitched by the gold-phantom then to consider any thing. Mack replied: "Probably a shaft must be sunk two thousand feet before the drift under the river-bed can be made; and your son, Tommy, will be a great-grandfather before the work may be accomplished. I prefer lighter and more accessible diggings."

"I must see that river of stone," said Virginia; "though amid its description I have been a journey upon memory's river. Just before we were graduated a classmate called at my room. Nothing could bring a smile to his face; and I urged him to let me share his trouble. He said: 'It is my chosen calling for life that almost unmans me—the ministry. If the leaders in Church affairs were like Christianity, loving and large-hearted, the people, who follow, would be likewise. But they sadly cramp ministers by captiousness, and doled salaries, and leaving to them many Church cares they would be happier and more useful to share. There are exceptional congregations, but unhappily the rule bears hardly upon ministers. In other professions equal attainments and toils lead to bountiful and pleasant surroundings for families. When my father, who was a minister, died, an old friend of his, not a member of the Church, proposed to put me through college, and give me time to repay his advances. He did it so nicely it would have been almost insulting to have declined. I received a letter from him to-day inclosing my notes receipted, and a sum of money besides, stating that he had heard I should preach, and it would help me start a library. I can accept neither the notes nor the inclosure. For apart from other reasons he has had reverses of late, and his family is large. But his letter has forever settled my purpose to preach. There may be many spirits like him; possibly I may be useful to some of them, and to others.'

"Two years after that I was visiting in a Kentucky village, and on Sabbath, to my joyful surprise, my old classmate rose in the pulpit. He closed the service by inviting to Church-membership. An old farmer was received into the Church, and said: 'Friends, from a child we have known this young man who has preached to us to-day. His father went up to heaven from amongst us, and when he died I determined to follow him as he followed Christ. I know I can never be like him; but help me to try.'

"I got my old classmate to dine with me; and when we entered our room he stood with his hand upon my shoulder, and said: 'Jack, he that joined the Church to-day is the man who helped me through college. I made by book-keeping money to pay him all he had advanced to me. When I took it to him, he said: "Frank, boy, don't do that. I can't take it. I have always wished to do something good; indeed, I think nearly everybody does. Don't *you* spoil my hopes, lad. When my little Carrie, your playmate, died, your father soothed her mother's heart and mine with many a kind word and delicate attention. And for the love I bear his memory, lad, let me have my way in this." So he placed the money in a small Testament, and gave it back to me, and said, The book is for your sister.'"

"And," added Virginia, "she is the blonde Kentucky girl I showed you, the other night, among the Sierra heights; and the book is *that* Testament. She said when she handed it to me: 'Jack, I only lend you this book; it's part of my heart; you must bring it back safe.'"

"I wish," said Tom, "Frank were here, and Leina, too. She would be delighted to meet him; her grandfather was a preacher.

"Whew!" said Pike, "that beats! What a fool, a-wishin' your wife were in the Sierry Mountains in the heart of this frizzen harricane to see Frank that ain't here, 'cause her grandpa were a parson, an' he the wanderin' son o' one."

In the instant that he closed his gibe, Pike emptied his revolver at objects we had neither heard nor seen, but amidst the "oughs" of retreating wolves one of them leaped upward and fell over dead in a few feet of the donkeys, and Pike added: "Thar's one o' them keerless prufessors now, Tom. Come help dash him in the gulf jest beyant him, or we'll hev more 'n him to kill afore day comes. For the rest on 'em will come back to eat him—they loves their like."

Tom heeded the counsel; and we were all soon asleep, regarding neither rush nor lull of the tempest.

CHAPTER XVIII.

TANGLED IN THE CORAL REEFS—'CEPT SHE'S POSSESST O' SATTAN.

HEN we awoke the sky was again clear, the morning-star sifted its purpling rays upon gray morn, and the sun, clinging to the tops of the crags, threw millions of sparkles upon the frosted jungle, till height and abysm appeared to be wrapped in a conflagration of ether. And as he pushed his face up full above the snow-crowns, and scattered his rays directer and warmer upon every thing, white vapors, like waves of bridal-veils, tangled in the tree-tops and unwinding from the icicles, wafted slowly up the iced crags, and drooping around them awhile floated on upward higher and higher into the bosom of the blue vault. But we had journeyed only a few miles ere the heavens were again overcast with hard, pale clouds that moved into position between us and the sun, till the canopy above and around us seemed to be a vast shroud

about us, and again we were whelmed in gusts of snow and sleet.

Pike said: "This are a suddint change. Roth, may be we've got into the windy sea o' Jewery that you talks about, specially ef you's scart and solemn, and are a-walkin' among its white waves in the foamy spray of one of its tempests, as you would say."

"I like that sea fancy," said Virginia; "the pale billows over us, the outspread sleet, the bottom of crumpling corals, the swimming snow-flakes drifting between, like polyps, wreathing garlands on coral tree and shrub and mound in the ether deep; and like divers seeking pearls, we grope in the white depths from object to object."

"But," said Mack, "I hope we shall be un-like some divers, who with handfuls of pearls get tangled in the coral reefs, and with glassy open eyes sleep forever in the bed of their gems, shrouded in their glitter. The tides chant chorals in the reefs, the busy polyps sing low, soft strains in the windows of the palaces of coral, and the pearls of great price are strewn about them; but the pale sleepers heed not the weird melodies, the charming dazzle, nor any glory."

"And," suggested Roth, "there are many,

though alive, faces still as stone, brain and heart stunned massing and summing gold, eyes glazy rays of eagerness for more, souls narrowed to the circle of its shine, blind to the true light, who neglect to buy of Jesus 'gold tried in the fire,' till death buries them in grasping the illusive riches that fail. How are we other than fatal blunderers who, for the treasures that flood us here, lose the heavenly that lie beyond the death-sea?"

We were grouped together the while in an open space, Roth between the donkeys leaning on one, his right-hand on the other's sedate brow. They seemed to be listening to us, our only auditors except the driving snow whose flakes appeared to ricochet above and about us, in many fantastic curves and twinkles, as if to put us in merrier mood. Heinrich seemed amazed by Roth's thought of any other gold than the visible, of any other life than the earthly; but Pike came to his relief by saying: "Tom 'minds me of two parsons I used to hear. One we called 'Blossom;' and he were a thumperer. I've heerd him lots. The beautifulest, unarthliest words you ever seed popped out 'n his lips, an' busted afore the crowd like a armful o' sky-rockets. He were edicated for a lawyer, an' come nigher makin' white black than arry judge you ever heern. He jumped about, run fore an' aft in the pulpit, turned up his eyes, rolled 'em, popped 'em, slung his voice up the mountain-top, an' d'rectly you'd hear it rumblin' in the chasm, and wonder how it got thar, an' what it were a doin' down thar 'mong all them arm-throwin's and unhuman gesturs an' figgers. He kivered his pint, ef he had any, with a bushel o' feathers, red, blue, black, white, yaller, spotted and streaked, so he never teched a targit.

"The other one we called 'Blunderbuss.' He were a sight. Ef you heern him once, you'd feel unarthly mean from head to heel, that ef you did n't change about you were goin' to Sattan an' no mistake; and I always noticed when he were done my heart were a-throbbin' arter a better life. But when Blossom were through sermontizin', I felt like I were tolerble good, a-needin' nothin' but wings to make me a angel."

"Dat vier goot," said Heinrich, "but ve is gone wrong. Drade-pose no dis way. Ve vier meucht loss in de stirm."

"Can't help it," answered Pike; "Virginny's got a little gold creetur that dances to the north star day and night, a lass give him. We are a-follerin' it for her sake; an' I never

knowed a addle-head man to go far wrong 'cept
he went contrary to women-kind. Foller a
woman-kind, 'cept she's possesst o' Sattan,
which ain't likely, an' you's sure to find yourself all right afore long."

"Adam no dinkt dat, when he tare through
der torns for doing like von vomins say."

"Adam," retorted Pike, "were wrong. He
ought to have staid more in her company, instid o' wanderin' round, like a Californy husband, leavin' her to the marcy o' Sattan. Ef
he'd staid at home, she'd a been all right
mebbe, an' we mought a been in the garden of
Eden to-day instid of in this whizzy snow an'
icy 'glommerations, as Tom calls the frizzen
things."

Tom winced a little, for he had been a long
time from his wife, and disliked the fragment-
ary style in which Pike quoted him. So he
said: "I said 'icy conglommerations;' and
Leina is as safe and happy where she is as if
I were there too."

"Yes," he rejoined; "an' more so. Ef she
wern't better nor a goddess, you'd 'ave gone
below to warm 'tarnally afore now. She are
the 'sprisenest creetur I ever see, only I never
seen her yet, to find any good or pritty about
you to 'maze her so. I know'd it were some

10

inhuman word stretchin' to sundown, without you wastin' the day in callin' it over. Ef Blossom ever gits that word, he 'll 'glommerate the folks with it till they 's deef enough not to hear a arthquake. Why did n't you say 'frizzen things,' then everybody would onderstand you?"

Tom moved on through the blasts without further parley; and about twilight next day we stretched a Norwegian tent, we had procured from a flitting company, amidst beautiful live-oaks on a point that a few feet from us dipped its granite face in the Stanislaus River, a few miles above Knight's Ferry.

The long, tortuous descent from the peaks and abysses of massy congelations had conducted us into a mild climate. The clouds broke in rain, or most of the feathery snowflakes, softening in the warmth of their fantastic mid-air waltz, rapidly dreamed themselves away as they swooned upon the sward. And contenting ourselves with mines bordering the valleys, though yielding but a few dollars a day, we gathered a few books and many newspapers about us, and forgot, in their light and peace, the dangers we had escaped.

CHAPTER XIX.

THE GLEAMING BLADE OF HIS NAKED BOWIE.

EINRICH, after a few weeks, departed for Stockton—or to get nearer an unfailing supply of lager, rather; and the restful scenes of the foot-hills becoming tame to us, Tom and Mack, and myself, went farther into the mountains prospecting.

The third night out we attended a mock temperance meeting. Perhaps two hundred men, belted with weapons and adorned with beards ten or twelve inches long, graced the occasion. The platform consisted of empty kegs, heads up. There were no seats; all stood. The president was a cool old sailor. A Dutchman, a Frenchman, a Michigander, and an Irishman, had spoken, extolling every drink except water amidst an uproar of applause.

When the fifth speaker ascended the kegs he was greeted with wildest huzzas; bottles peeped from his pockets, and his voice, as he acknowledged the honor, was akin to the tremolo key of an organ out of tune. He emptied a bottle at a draught, while the crowd gathered closer about him, and said: "Gentlemen and ladies."

"Hello, Kaintuck!" yelled an Irishman, "tharre's not one o' the last sax herre."

"Well," he answered, "there ought to be in this *dacent* company, surely."

"Say ladies and gentlemen, then, Commodore!" exclaimed many voices.

He uncorked his second bottle and took a long drink. The fluid gurgled, gurgled down his throat. All eagerly watched him till, as the bottle tilted to a perpendicular between his teeth, some cried out: "He's good as dead, boys! That's too much for two *sober* men."

"Who says 'good as dead?'" he asked, dropping the bottle at his feet. "Is it intemperance that destroys? When did that become an article of faith with you? It is temperance that palsies the nerves, loosens the joints, unstrings the muscles, gives the body a zigzag motion, numbs the brain, deadens the kindlier feelings of the heart, and wakes up fiends in it.

"It is temperance that quarrels with the best friend, spends all its store in rioting, feeds on hunger, clothes in rags, beats woman, breaks her loving heart, frightens children and makes them weep when God intended their little faces should be brave as innocence, and smile like cherubim.

"It is temperance that poisons the blood, bloats the form, gives wounds and bruises without cause, reddens the eye and blears its vision; fouls the air with profanity, mocks sacred things, guillotines honor, provokes discord, stirs to murder, wrecks energy, stifles independence, and disgraces a State by adding to its prison registry a long list of dishonored names.

"It is temperance that taxes the sober for the drunken, the pure and peaceable for the fiendish, and turns grain needed for the hungry into liquor that laughs at calamity and sows sorrows. It transmutes wisdom into insanity, and stripping the soul of all that's purest and best in the casket of immortality, leaves it mean, and virtueless, and fitted for perdition. It twines gray hair with woes, fills sweet old mother's heart with floods of desolate grief; and opens an early grave, a grave of shame, a pauper's grave, a grave of crime, a grave over which no sigh that the buried one is gone ever sheds its pathetic murmur."

During his speech the crowd had become still as a desert, and from the moment that he dropped his bottle his voice was musical and clear. Each phrase was articulate irony whose presence, like electricity, was felt by his auditors. But if they strove at all to shake off its spell, they utterly failed, till the speaker stood mute, pale, watching a boy just in the teens pressing to the platform. There was a deathly pallor on the lad's face as he stepped to his side, and the voice was inimitably tender as he said: "Father, please go to the tent."

"Certainly, my boy; yes, at once."

The boy whirled upon his heel, facing the wild crowd, and said: "You are fiends!"

I saw Tom move close to him; but had no time to think. Several were already yelling, "Knock that boy on the head! down with him!"

He did not quail, but said: "I say it again. You are fiends! You are making mockery of my good father. You have led him to drink again, and brought him to this accursed company to make sport, by his eloquence, for your sottish souls."

Angry voices railed at him again, and I saw the old man fingering his bowie. A half dozen irritated men were approaching him, when a clear voice rang across the cursing throng: "The boy shall speak! Touch him who dares!"

I knew the voice at its first note for Tom's, but its silvery defiance had scarcely split the air before blows, like the thuds of the catapult, were falling, that made the heart sicken and rage. Presently the thoughtful men present had secured a truce, but not before Roth and Mack who had sprung to his side had felled several of the chief assailants.

The president, when the truce obtained, was sitting precisely as he was when the first blow was struck; but the old man, whose speech had been interrupted, was standing upon the first row of kegs with his left arm tightened round the boy, a little in advance; and the gleaming blade of his naked bowie glittered in his steady right-hand. No eye that beheld him then but knew that to touch that boy was death; and the reckless revelers, as the posture caught their glance, involuntarily cheered, till the old Kentuckian, becoming conscious of the heroic tableau he was presenting, placed the boy on a cask and sat down by him.

The first word, after the fight was checked, was from Tom, of course. I expected him to be shot every moment. He had planted himself in the very tracks he stood in when the first blow was struck, and, exactly in the same key as before, said: "The boy shall speak!"

"No," said the old man, jumping to his feet, "he has said enough. And, friends, I regret to have occasioned any thing unpleasant. Many of you know how ruinous to me intemperance has been. I am sober, have not tasted liquor in five months; hope never to again. The bottles you saw me use held only lemonade. My intention was to have made you a temperance speech in *my* way, when my boy's face amazed me coming through the crowd; and knowing how he was suffering because, like you, he thought me again drinking, I lost my self-poise. Your president knew my plan, and approved it. Let me be done with it, by expressing the wish that you will all be friends, and join with me in exiling your palates from whisky forever."

As he ceased, the old sailor rapped with his big jack-knife on a cask, and said: "Round to thar; round to, my hearties! Come to order. If you'll say *intemperance* whar Commodore Kaintuck said temperance you'll have his spache as he mint it. You're bound to have your fun. But as cap'n of this ship, I say throw o'erboard such lumber as making sport of a good thing, and quit grog, or you will go down, under full sail, to blue blazes. I declar this meetin' 'jarned over to, to, to judgment-day."

On our return to camp Roth discovered that he had swallowed a tooth, and maintained that my skull had knocked it out, trying to get from the fighting circle. Professing to be a boxing expert, he disliked to own to a square blow from an antagonist; but the only blow he could give was one at a venture, and his skill in fencing was to receive a blow on the spot it was aimed at.

Finding a rich gulch among the taller foothills, we located claims; and Roth and the brown donkey went to pilot the gray donkey and Pike and Virginia to the placer.

CHAPTER XX.

O IT WAS A SWEET, PURE FACE!—EVERY THING BUT LIFE, THE DANCE OF LIFE.

UR new camp was in a sequestered portion of the jungle. The hills about us, however, were generally less than five hundred feet above us, and were inlaid and underlaid by gray rocks whose brows, when long exposed, had become dark and rent and rugged. The placer broke away from the abrupt base of one of the lower hills, and was divided in its length by a branch whose supplies of water, when the winter rains had ceased, we increased by uncapping several springs and turning their streams to that of the placer. The fall in the water channel was comparatively great, and, together with the narrowness of the hill-pent mine, made our labor the less worrying; and the gravel "panned out" richly, and the bed-rock richer. So we were contented to cheerfully "pitch in;" and as the fine days of approaching spring flooded us with sunshine, to break the weeping spells of dying winter,

wo were fairly rid of the gloom the hard winter had imparted to us.

In those days a fine suit of clothes was scarcely ever seen in the mines. We were surprised by the appearance of one such, at our tent door one evening, piloted by a miner we had met on the Stanislaus. But when we beheld the joyful greeting with which Rothleit welcomed its wearer, we were satisfied to have it about. He was an old law friend of Roth's, from New York, called to California in the interest of some large old Mexican land grants; and wishing to see the mines, before returning east, was pushing south to the Fremont Claim, which was then exciting some stir. Chancing to hear of Roth through the miner, whom he had met in the stage, he had turned aside to greet him.

He spent two or three days with us; renewed his boyhood rifle-practice by some successful shots at deer that were now gliding back to the mountains from the valleys; and blistered his hands mining for nuggets, to show to friends at home as having been dug by himself from the gold-fields. He was a genial visitor, and imparted to us a wishfulness for the soft garbs, the nice conventionals, the civilized surroundings of the Atlantic Coast; but this died out in a few days, and we and the gold-phantom were cousinly as ever. Tom staged it with him to the head of the Mariposas, and kept us awake many hours, the night he got back to the tent, by his restlessness and narratives, bringing the light of the snow-crags about us again. He said:

"Snow-man was a passenger with me in the journey back to the Stanislaus crossing, bound for Jamaica, his home. He has been fairly successful, and will sail from San Francisco in two or three days. The story he told us at Tempest Camp was not all the truth; miner-like, he concealed the golden reason of his being lost. He and the Mexican had mined together. Afterward, in a fandango, he had struck aside a pistol from his heart, not an instant too soon; for the bullet plowed under his skin, and fired his clothes. He had shown real gratitude; and, after a separation of months, had arranged, by letter, to meet him at a trading-post ten miles west of Tempest Camp, to direct him to a rich gulch. Snow-man had purposely turned from the hunting party, but losing his way, had failed to meet him till they unexpectedly met at our camp. The Mexican observed when I withdrew from the tent in the storm, and awoke him; and when they were without the tent, induced him to

leave at once, to return early in the morning.
The plea was that he knew the jungle so well
that he could thread it safely, and that his
brother awaited him in camp a mile or two
away, to start with him back to Sonora, Mexico,
whence they had come, and was fearfully uneasy, as he was a day or two behind time. As
they groped their way, he detailed to him how
to find and know the gulch, which was fifty
miles off. They slept at a brush tent, under a
cliff with another Mexican; but when he awoke
next morning he was alone, and not a trace of
the Mexicans to indicate the direction they had
taken. In seeking to find us, he luckily wandered toward the valley, and so escaped the
fearful experiences that had tortured us. He
had mined the gulch that paid largely.

"At the foot of a beautiful mountain we left
the stage, with other passengers, to walk on by
a trail, while it made a circuit to avoid some
rough ravines. The day was charming; the
sleepy sunshine threw a soft trance upon every
thing. The mahogany-hued manganites, the
low-branched oaks, the winding trail, the old
gray great rocks, the pebbly gulches, the
mountains with their shadowy labyrinths, the
songful birds, the plumy flowers resting their
cheeks upon the ether, or dallying with the

grass, were suggestive of peace and life. But a few steps farther brought us in the shadow of an oak upon whose boughs two human forms hung. They were Mexicans, and we stepped beneath the tree to examine the dead sons of an evil destiny.

"As they turned to and from each other in the noiseless waltz of death, in mid-air, one swung lower than the other. He was poorly clad, of graceful build, and appeared to be a man of toil. His head, as he swung to and fro solemnly, then spun round and round slowly, as the zephyrs played with his hair, inclined a little to one side and drooped. A soft expression ineffably sad, resigned, forgiving, mourning in itself in utter helpless friendlessness, was upon his dusky countenance, and on his placid brow innocency was so plainly writ in death's strange letters that we marveled why He, without whom not a sparrow dies, had yielded him to so sorrowful a fate. O it was a sweet, pure face, looking as though innocence, in unpitied heart-break, had painted herself there, and died!

"The other was neatly dressed. A miner's shirt of green flannel, jacket-like; black cassimere trousers, clasped round his waist by a bright leathern girdle; a flaunty necktie, and fine, close-fitting boots, all new, were his costume. His head was erect; his face bloated as from recent debauch, was contorted with stark horror, while in every lineament were coiled masses of snakish hate and guilt. His brow was corrugated, and a hideous scowl upon it seemed to be communing with many murders. His dead eyes were wide open, fixed in dread gaze, as if on appalling specters flitting with his bodeful soul. No one who looked upon him but felt that his, though a stern, was a just doom.

"It seemed to me that I had seen him before, and as we moved on to meet the coach, memory was busied with many faces, when Snow-man said: 'That's the Mexican you charged with murder the night of the storm in the mountains; the fiendish-looking one back yonder, hanging highest. I have never seen nor heard of him since then until now. What a horrible face! and yet he had been grateful to me.'"

"And assassinous to me," said Virginia, interrupting the narrative.

"We learned at the next stage-stand," continued Tom, "that they had been lynched the night before, as one was a notorious robber and murderer, and the other had interfered to save him, and was treated as his accomplice. Judge Lynch, specially when in a hurry, is sure to blunder till at his illegal hands sometimes the comparativly guiltless suffer the doom of the guiltiest."

"In a soul," said Mack, "close together imps and angels abide. They strive with each other, and, the soul's nature being like the imps, these hold it until one mightier than imps and angels comes—the Christ; then the imps must go, or the soul. If it persist for the imps, it is loosed by the Great King to mate with them only, and together they hurry to the fearful doom of sin. If the Mexican had heeded that angel, Gratitude, till its pure calls had gathered to him penitence, faith, hope, love, his life would have been a thing so useful and noble that though his death had been by violence, by the sins of others, it would have been peaceful to him. But instead, his life was corrupted more and more as he harbored added imps, and none can ever know here the evil that he did. His poor friend's death, as his own, evidently was caused by his life of crime. What a curse is a wicked life!"

"And how disastrous often," said Virginia, "one evil life is to another! and quickly comes the disaster! I knew ———, in the ———. mines, a reticent, courteous young man. Those who knew him in his tropic home, ere he

touched this shore that infatuates so many
with the vices of gaming and drink, tell many
pleasant things of him. In a dance-house,
over a mountain whose blue top and green
sides witch the eye, he chanced to overhear a
curse a Mexican breathed against Americans.
Pausing in the dance, he resented it by a slap
in the face; but meeting no resistance, he
turned away, and again was whirling in the
frantic pleasure of the waltz. The flush upon
his cheek was rosy with life, the eye glowy
with delight; and care had fled to to-morrow
from the thrill of music and motion. The
magnetism of the sensual revel suffused him
body and soul with its sensuous spell, till
every thing but life, the dance of life, was a
whisk of nothingness to him. The crack of a
pistol at the door, a thud to the floor of his
form from the whisking circle, a gush of blood
from the white bosom, a convulsive shudder, a
gurgling gasp, and life was gone—his eyes
stretched after his ghost gliding away from the
quivering company. A minute before the in-
sulted Mexican had crouched, from the scene
of light and life, into the darkness, and sent
death to take his place within, whilst he fled
deeper into the mountains. Several days
passed; but the friends of the slain man were

11

busy. One evening he watched the red sun
burying himself in the distant sea of valleys,
and turning down the shrubby height was pen-
etrating to a tall pine whose brow glowed with
the purple of sundown painting cliffs and
rocks and thicket and firmament. Every
object seemed breathless with joy. The red
manganites, robed in silvery foliage rubied
with sky glints, were motionless with excess of
peace; the birds were at rest upon the golden
leaf-cups, viewing the blush of bush and air
ere fluttering to sleep for the night; and the
wild deer paused as they crept from their
coverts, marveling at the red flush suffusing
every thing. He looked sad, as though death
spoke to him from the crimson wave of clouds
in which the sun had buried himself; and as
he edged the chasm to near the pine, to obtain
tidings and provisions from his friends, he
halted and peered about, glided on, paused,
watching in the soft twilight like a startled
panther, fearing, about to go back, pondered,
then on again a few hesitating steps, and listened alert, as if foreboding ill. Blue puffs
whiffed up in the ether, a volley of fire-arms
crashed among the shrubs, its black smoke like
veils of crape floated upon the ruby thicket, a
husky groan from a dusky form writhing in

blood upon the sward; a few men rose up from among the rocks, painted by the ghost of the buried sun as they grouped where the smoking blood lay curdling, and the dead man's stare and ashy face told them how true their aim had been. So crimes followed crime. And evermore it is so until He who 'stopped dying to save a soul' takes sin away."

CHAPTER XXI.

DRESS AN ISTHMUS MONKEY.

HE moonless night sprinkled with stars was dozing upon the lone mountains, and we caught the silence of the solitude as we thought of Tom's narrative. Nor did our improvised stone lounges seem hard to us, for we had just read "letters from home" that he had brought from the post; and were languidly puffing some rare Havanas, dreaming dreams and seeing visions of the persons and objects in our dear old home across the continent.

However, Mack presently broke up our reverie by reading to us the following letters from Clay S—— and Wyche L——, who had mined with him soon after he came to California. They had gone back home, but reminded Mack of their miner-life by an occasional letter. Clay's was as follows:

"——, KENTUCKY, —— 13, —.

"*Dear Mack:* I have been married ever since I got back from the gold-fields, nine months and twenty-seven days, about. You have seen Minnie's picture, so I need not describe her to you, only she has been growing in beauty and goodness to me, from our marriage-eve. This morning she is very, very beautiful.

"The baby is two weeks and five days old, and now sleeps upon her arm under a rainbow of smiles reflected from her face. And, Mack, there is no mistake about it, the baby is incomparably pretty and smart. From present indications, we think he is destined to exceed 'Harry of the West' himself, for whom I am named, in stateliness of form, wisdom, sprightly wit, and eloquence. Were you to see him as he lies in ribbons and ruffles, looking about at things, I know you would agree to what I say. He had a glorious red color the first few days of his life. We were very much delighted, Minnie and I. For we expected he would grow up real rosy, graceful, and plump, instead of bony, impish-looking, like other boys. But after two or three days he began to whiten in spots, which made us very uneasy; for we feared very much he was taking the leprosy, which you know whitens one wonderfully.

"Minnie discovered it first, and was near going distracted about it at once. For her mother's favorite darky, old Aunt Hetty, as kind a nurse as ever stole sugar for the children, or danced at a Christmas frolic, has been turning white in splotches the last twenty years; and Minnie said she knew the baby would look just that way when he was a man—a streak of white and a streak of red, like old Hetty, a streak of white and a streak of black.

"We sent for the doctor, who told us when he came that it was nothing much, yet not entirely usual; but that the child was so uncommon anyhow we might expect unusual things of him; to watch closely, and if he whitened regularly, only here and there a tinge of pink, it was all right.

"He left a small vial of some colorless fluid, tasteless unless it tasted like water, with directions to give ten drops of it to the baby every five hours, when awake, till the sixth day, and by that time he would be a soft, natural, creamy white. And it was so. And I advise you, if you ever have a child that's very red for a few days after birth, to send for Dr. ——, or one of his pupils, at once. We like the fair skin of the baby better, I believe, than we did its color—red—before we sent for the doctor, thanks to him.

"Minnie's mother says that the whitening was all natural, that Minnie herself was the reddest thing alive when only one or two days old. But she's a great talker any way.

"His head, the baby's, is round, except it may bulge somewhat behind, and his hair is already nearly black. We are glad that's so; for we talked it over, and agreed that we never could stand it if he were to have a white head. The hair is soft as floss of silk. Short neck, long eyelashes, blue, flashy eyes, and about them, too, is a most deep, profound look that denotes genius. The doctor seems to agree with us in that; especially my wife's mother and mine do. His nose is a fac-simile Grecian nose; I wish you could see it. His cheeks are plump, a little red yet; and his ears are the most symmetrical I ever beheld. His mouth is a rare grace; it puckers, a little I mean, and large with thick lips—I do not mean much so, just enough so to resemble the grand 'Harry.' His chin curves, indicative of masculinity, and is dimpled. His arms and legs are exquisite models; so Minnie and I think, and are sustained in the opinion by Minnie's *old college mates*—so she tells me; *they* have been very kind in calling to see him.

"We thought yesterday he had a tooth coming through; but the doctor said he thought not, as children were seldom so smart as to cut teeth under three months old; and as our boy is not three weeks old, it's possible that we are mistaken. His hands and feet are small, the sign of *blood*. Indeed, Mack, he's the handsomest, most perfect child, I ever heard of. Minnie says that all the ladies who have called, and they are many, say that he is the prettiest, cunningest—they mean intelligent —and finest-looking child they ever saw. We are greatly troubled about naming him. I prefer Washington Greene Gates, after the three most distinguished generals of the Revolutionary War. Minnie inclines to Æsop Cicero; but she's afraid the impish boys, when he goes to school, will call him Sis, or Sop; and she never could stand that. And she says that Aunt Clink says that if she consents to the name I have chosen, the boys will call him nothing but Greene Gates.

"Uncle Tobe says that we are the two biggest fools in America, and he'll bet his blue-grass farm against a blue paper of pins that the child will be a bigger fool than both of us put together. But he's an old fossil, so you needn't believe what he says about the baby.

.   .   .   .

"I have had to stop writing to consult about the boy's name. We have agreed to name him

Tobias De Wittle, after Uncle Tobe, who is clever as they make 'em even in Kentucky. He said this morning that we were exactly right—that there never was such another baby in the world as ours, who has certainly grown nearly an inch since yesterday."

This letter is scarcely in accord with the extract below from a letter of his Cousin Wyche. And not being equal to view the difference in "a dry light," what could we do but leave it where we found it? Wyche wrote:

"I shall be in California again in two months. Called the other day to see Clay. His wife is rarely beautiful. How she ever fancied Clay is an enigma; perhaps amiability, courtesy, and business habits make a man, however ruggedly featured, handsome in woman's estimate. They have a boy baby now of whom they are very proud. Clay gave me a voluble account of his perfections, before taking me to the crib to see him. Of course I could say nothing to discount a grace, however imaginary, from the little fellow. It takes *something* to set me back, you know; but I met something in that child. Mack, he's the ugliest thing in mortal shape. I was amazed at the sight. His head is long and one-sided; hair, tow-colored; ears, purple and large like a valley rabbit's; frog-eyed; his nose, like a flat piece of fresh beef dumped carelessly just over his mouth in which he was cramming both hands; and he screwed his face till I drew back, fearing he was about to turn outside in. If you would dress an Isthmus monkey in a slim ruffle-shirt, wrap it up in white flannel rimmed with pink ribbon, and wash its face in chalk and red paint mixed, and mash its foot till its face was set to a hundred screeches, you would have as fair a picture of Clay's baby as can be given. But I believe babies are all alike, only this one is more like the ugly of all the rest."

By the time the reading was finished Pike had a midnight stew of canned oysters ready, and said: "Virginny, pass them ar iceters to Clay's baby."

Virginia thought a moment, then plumped the stew-pan down by Tom, who quietly emptied about half the oysters into his prospecting pan, and ate them, filing no disclaimer to his baby-hood.

"Waal," drawled Pike, "your handsome par will be arter you d'rectly with a tumbler full o' paregoric. You are bound to be collict."

But he wasn't.

CHAPTER XXII.

OUT OF WHICH CAME TO US SORROWFUL
WHISPERS.

THE banks of the mine grew taller and more rugged with jutting rocks, as we pushed the pit nearer the base of the hill. And as the warmth of April played with the snow that yet capped the highest hills about us, the days were balmy, though fresh and cool; while the nights were so' cold that we kept good fires, in whose winking light we told stories of the past, or interchanged thoughts. As he leaned against the tent-pole, propped upon his elbow, musing, Pike said: "When I were wounded in Mexico, and left by the doctors to die afore mornin', a little pale-face man, that looked like a corpse, crawled off his pallet to me, and nursed me all night. Once, when the spasms wrung me so I thought I was a-goin', he wiped the death-sweat from my face with the nicest part o' his shirt-sleeve, and put his hand upon my heart. A minute arterwards I missed him, and looked about for him best I could, for I shuddered to die by myself. I saw him crawlin' away fast as he could out o' the dingy room, but d'rectly he were back ag'in with a red-face surgeon I never see afore. He said to me: 'Comrade, never give up till it's all over. This doctor will watch with me, and if there's a chance you'll be all right yet.' He drug his pallet close to mine, and they got me and mine onto it gently as they could, so I could die safter. But they kept tryin' to better me, ontil in a day or two I were improvin', and in a month were ready for to march. I used to go to my old pallet-place, and hobble along the track o' blood that flowed from his own wound, as he crawled arter the doctor to come help him revive me, and wonder whar he were. The watchers had told me that he were removed one night while I were out o' my head, and he were delirious, too, and they had to force him away; and that's all I could larn about him. Arter that, in the battle o' Molino del Rey, I saw a soldier cheering a company that were waverin'. He said, 'Never give up till it's all over;' and a shot cut him down afore you could say huzza. But I knowed him by them words. When the order come to move position, I sprung over the ditch frontards into the corn whar he were a-lyin' dead-like, and bore him along with us. The captain told me to carry him out o' danger, and come back at double-quick. He groaned a time or two, as I were a-toatin' of him, so I knowed he wern't quite dead; and when I laid him down among t'others where the doctors was a-cuttin' of 'em wus, gougin' for the bullets in 'em, I gave him some water and bathed him off. When he come to, I said: 'An' yer do n't know me?' 'No,' he said, 'but I will; my head ain't just right yet.' 'Yes,' said I, 'but yer heart will do to bet on any time. Do n't you mind in Jalapa a-crawlin' arter a doctor one night, fur a fursaken fellow gin up to die, and bleedin', as you crawled, puddles of blood from your own wounds?' 'Ah!' he answered, 'it's Jim; glad you got well. I'm sick, sick;' and he fainted away suddint ag'in.

"It were worth while to be thar, to see the glitter o' joy on his filmy eye when he called me Jim; but he were mistaken. I told him, arter he got 'most well, my name wern't Jim, but Racket; for I knowed some secret were on his heart that warmed it wrongly to me. 'Well,' he said, 'you are just like Jim Knight who dragged me from under the Mexican spears after we were both wounded, when Col. Clay was killed, and brought me safe off the field.'

But he never told me he got wounded under them lances a-savin' Jim's life, but I knowed it, for Jim were my twin brother, and when he told me about it, he said: 'And Racket, ef ye ever can get a chance to do Sam M—— a good turn, lad, put him through heart-like; bless him, Racket, kinder like mother would bless him.' And Jim were in arnest about then, for his tender, true hand were on my shoulder, and a tear were in his eye when he said it. Anyhow I double-quicked round Sam instid o' back, for the battle were won afore we got out o' range; and he were fightin' a battle now all alone with death, and I tried to make one with Sam ag'in death; and he pulled through; and I toated him out o' the hospital one day and laid him down on some fresh fodder under a tree. He were crazy enough for awhile, but he slept mighty deeply presently, and woke up while I were a-lookin right into his face; and he smiled, and said, 'Jim.' 'No,' said I; 'Racket *for* Jim.' 'Well,' said he, 'it's both.' 'Yes,' said I, 'for me and Jim is one for such a fellow as Sam M——, forever. Now sleep ag'in, and git well to rescue some more o' your comrades. "Never give up till it's all over." I'm a-goin' to be right by you, Sam; sleep—sleep.' And he did, and got well at last. Marssy, boys, to be clever were or'nary with that pale scrap of a man. He'd give his blood for a comrade any day."

Here Pike's eye wandered over a broadcloth suit athwart the projecting end of the rib-pole of the tent above him, whither Tom had tossed it the week before, when he got back from his Mariposa trip. The fragrant smoke of our Havanas, gray streaked with thin blue, hugged it coquettishly ere twirling higher in the air that seemed to stretch its laughing eyes upon it, too; and he said: "Tom, you brought a armful o' newspapers, an' five boxes o' cigars, and that *cloth suit* up thar you is so keerful of, when you come back from Mariposa. You are bound to be rich a-goin' on in that style. The Gov'ment ought to 'pint you univarsal spendthrift, to show now big a blossom in that line Ameriky kin grow."

Tom ground the end of his cigar between his teeth, and hurried up two or three puffs of smoke, but said nothing. He had often insisted, in his series of camp-fire lectures, that neither of us knew aught of economy but himself; and that fine suit, that we had already made a towel of on occasions, gave Pike a chance to retaliate, too good to let slip; and he continued: "You need them ar sort o' clothes,

puddling in the mud and water waist deep
every day mining, an' you hangs 'em thar to
show 'the fitness in things,' as you say."

Tom flipped the spire of ashes off his cigar,
and replied: "I felt shabby in miner's garb
with my New York friend, and a clever gentleman told me he was selling off at cost, in Mariposa, and let me have the suit for eighty dollars—it was priced at a hundred."

"Yes," said Pike, "that clever gentleman
were marciful to you; he made you pay only
thirty dollars more 'n anybody else."

"Nearer forty," he answered, owning he had
been overreached ere he thought, "as I discovered on pricing suits for Snow-man at another store. But I 'll trade with him no more."

"No," said Pike, "but you will with some
other clever gentleman till you are no more, or
your gold's all gone, for all your lecturs to the
balance on us about prudence, and 'conomy,
as you call being stingy."

Pike's case against him was too clear for
Tom to rally, and he good-humoredly beat a
retreat into the realms of reverie; and the camp
was still as the snow yet crowning a mountain,
that overtopped the taller hills or spurs just
about us, and appeared in the sky-shine like a
white cloud sleeping upon a long, high bed of

ebony. Pike said:¯ "Boys, that mountain 'minds me of a monster giant dead, under a shroud too narrow to kiver him round good. I've been reading Tom's Bible. Somebody's marked a varse which reads, 'Be ye therefore ready also, for in such an hour as ye think not the Son of man cometh.' More'n twenty folks I've known in this country was called aboard the death-ship suddint-like. Ef I'm overtook anywhars near you, don't let me be buried like a hithen. Send for a parson, and have a hime an' a prayer at my grave, or read 'em yourselves, ef he can't be got. It will be more comfort to my mother's good heart, in old Missouri, when she hears on it than 'most any thing else. I have sent her nigh onto ten thousand dollars to have for her own; and she writ me six months ago not to trouble about sendin' her any more, for she had more'n would make her comfortable."

The solemnity of Pike's manner, perhaps more than his words, impressed us; and somehow every eye was on his face when his voice hushed. We knew it was a kind, brave face that twitched with sympathy for every thing true and good, and that weakness and suffering could not look to it without being blessed, and with a niceness almost as rare as delightful.

12

It was earnest and quiet and sad, as his voice had been. But presently we all slept, and the dreams of the night, and the brightness of the day that followed, put away from our minds the soft words he had spoken. The second day, however, Mack and Virginia went hunting, and I lingered about the tent. On looking toward the mine, an hour before noon, I saw Tom staggering toward me with a man in his arms. When I met him, he said: "He's gone, Quien; bank caved in on him!"

As I helped to lay Pike upon a blanket under shelter of an oak near the stream, I saw, indeed, he was quite dead. His back was broken, his breast crushed; besides, there was a mortal contusion of the skull. I asked Tom why he didn't come for me to help bring him to the tent?

"I tried to," he replied, "but I couldn't. I couldn't leave him down there by himself, though I knew he was dead. He never spoke, never breathed that I could see, after the great rock rolled over him. But, Quien, he looked like he was still alive; his lips appeared parting to utter some pleasantry, and the old smile preparing to send its ripples over his face. All the morning he has been even more buoyant than usual. What a bubble is life! We scarce see its form fully on the river of time ere, shattered by the unexpected blast, it disappears. It is like the music of a rill, barely heard ere it is hushed in the folds of the sighing wind forever."

A Tennessee parson, who occasionally had shared our camp in the foot-hills, read the burial-service descriptive of the resurrection; and piling over the place large rocks, that the coyotes and wolves should haunt it to no purpose, we left our genial, fearless comrade alone in the shadow of the great hill, in a cluster of manzanita whose shiny limbs formed about him a dense hedge.

But at the tent that night something was missing. The humorous gibe, the tender story uniquely told, the hopeful words, the soft though gleeful laugh, the gray eye that talked more than the tongue, the inhering courtesy that as naturally considered and conferred joy upon others as the diamond shines, the broad-breasted, tall form with womanly heart, of unpretentious courage, was gone. And in the tent, and around the fire without, and in the shadow next the thicket, there seemed visible a space in the spaces, where Pike was wont to be, out of which came to us sorrowful whispers constantly bewailing his absence.

And we talked of the pale one in the thicket of the dead. And mayhap you will not be repelled by our weakness when you read that hardened as we were, by *rough scenes in the mines that I hide from you*, as we thought and talked of him, one and another would turn his face to the dark, and try to repress the weeping that would sob in our hearts for him.

However, after awhile Virginia said: "Once I stood next the guards of a palace-steamer far out at sea. The breath upon the deep was soft, the fathomless waters still and clear. The ship was at rest like a white fragment of sky on the quiet wave; its flag of stars and stripes drooped at half-mast like glory lamenting misfortune. Upon a plank lay a young physician who the day before was rosy with life. The cholera had stricken him down in the presence of his wife while, with a thousand others, they were voyaging to the golden shore. A sail was wrapped and sewed tightly round his body, leaving exposed only his head and face; a mass of stone-coal was bound to his feet, and his hair lay smoothed back from his dead face. About him many passengers were grouped— on the wheel-house, on the deck, upon chairs, or benches, or rope-coils they stood, awed; for among them the noiseless plague was passing to and fro, and already scores of the company had shivered into death at its touch. The plank was tilted by two sailors, and the doctor glided feet-foremost down into the deep blue sea a few fathoms, and paused a moment, sunk deeper, paused, then deeper, and quivered and stood erect, motionless; buried at sea. The steam - whistle wailed, the bell tolled, strong men sighed, the machinery groaned, the engine awoke the wheels to rapid evolutions, the steamer moved on, and in the vibratory waters the doctor, down in his clear, blue grave standing, bowed again and again, his back to us—a 'good-by' from the dead to the living. And then he was alone waiting there—waiting, deaf to every sound save that trumpet signal that sea and earth shall hear, and lift to their bosom all their dead children, to be caught up to meet the Lord in the air. To be buried in the sea of waters, or beneath the motionless rocks in the sea of mountains, what does it matter, so our houses of silence shall echo in the morning of Christ with salvation's sound? Shall we be 'ready' when he cometh?"

Education has much to do with reputation, if not with character as well. It is a refining basanite. Pike had never polished under its culturing touches, but such was the native princeliness of his taste, impulse, and manner, such the brimful sprightliness and force of his mind, and so high-graded his emotions, that he had twined himself around our hearts like the vine of pure gold round the column of the sacred temple at Jerusalem. And when Virginia's story closed, Tom's face lit up with something like a blush, and he said: "When Leina consented for me to come to the gold-fields, she wept so much that in trying to soothe her I promised to adore God about twilight every day. She as much expects me to do so as she expects the devil not to be a saint; and I have disappointed her in so many things, if she could believe it, that I am trying not to in this. One twilight as we came down the mountains, last winter, Pike entered the icy thicket and quietly knelt near me, as he did daily thereafter till his death. We never exchanged a remark concerning the habit all the months we observed it together. He said shortly after we opened this mine: 'My heart is a surprise to me. Its hates are gone; peace and love make me glad all the time; and I think of God, eternity, and death with hope, without dread. My little sister Jule, who went to heaven when we were children together, has latterly come tripping about me in my sleep, and played with my hair as she used to in life; and last night when she left me she beckoned me to follow, and said, Soon. So she 'll come for me before long; and it 's all right *here*, Tom, right with the heart. It loves the earth and its folks, and would be glad to throb a long while among 'em; but it loves heaven and its angels, and believes it 's a-goin' there to be among 'em forever.' "

Mack and I went up to the gray rocks lying upon Pike's grave. The night was bright with the April skies. The air was fresh, though nearly motionless. In the dell, at the campfire, Virginia and Tom chatted, and now and then their voices broke upon the cairn where we sat like the monotones of invisibles. Huge rocks lay in enchanted meditation on shrubless knolls, and the raylets twinkled merrily upon their wrinkled faces. The hazy patches of chaparral on the mountain over the hills peered from their lonesome beds into the somber ravines whose brinks they bordered; and thirty feet from us a leafy covert quivered and bent about quietly, then was at rest again; and another farther on did likewise, and yet others; it was only the muffled zephyr greeting them on its journey from sea to mountain, and passed on, climbing down gorges, up precipices, over heights, and away, away. A hundred feet above us, and as many yards beyond, a streamlet tossed about on sleepless bed, and drummed hurried strains to air and plant and mossy shore, then leaped into the chasm, and floated up clouds of spray that hung above its splash, like a snowy veil woven for its bridal with the valley. Just at us a water-oak stood stretching one budding branch, like a hand of blessing, over Pike's cairn, and its twigs glided repeatedly as if fanned aside by a gentle sprite in noiseless ramble o'er the scene. The crickets chirped in the brush-wood, and near the roots of the tree glow-worms kindled their pale fires. A fawn bounded across a clear space into a shadowy one, and hied to a dense thicket, and a moment later a coyote leaped after it, and a startled rabbit sped to the cairn and hid at our feet. From the many-voiced streamlet, and thousands of twiggy lutes and rocky harps, Æolian hymns—low, adoring, reverential— mingled with the seeming hum of the worshiping stars, till the jungle, the dead under the cairn, and the living above it, were lost from thought, and only God appeared.

Mack seemed to have observed the scene closely, for he said: "This is a phase of earth's night-life, in the golden solitude, that is en-

trancing. Yet just now an innocent fawn was
fleeing from covert to covert for life, and a
harmless rabbit fled from its burrow to escape
death there, and hid here in Pike's cairn, where
it trembles at every softest sound as if it shall
be its death-knell. Is death everywhere, pursuing every thing, nor resting at midday nor
midnight? What is it, that all animated nature pales in its breath, perishes in the way if
but touched by it? As it relates to man, is it
the ceasing to be of his being? Then that
heart-flower, immortality, is a dream; and
those brilliant devils Voltaire and Robespierre
—calling massacre justice, the guillotine gentle
mercy, and the submergence of religion and
liberty in the red floods of tyranny patriotism,
death an eternal sleep —were the world's bene-
factors; and the lessons of the good Christ were
dreamy lies. To believe that is to lodge in the
soul the most preposterous absurdity. And
yet the fact recurs, death is. What is it? It
comes slowly sometimes, like the invincible
soldier mining the citadel's foundation; swiftly
sometimes, like the cloud's bolt; and the ear
becomes deaf, the eye blind, the lips dumb, the
brain, the heart, the body still, and we bury
or burn it, or leave it unurned to bleach to
dust in the weather of ages. But ourself, the

soul, eternity's heir, still lives, waiting in the mysterious shade beyond death to hear the voice of Christ reuniting it and its body to assign it its eternal destiny."

CHAPTER XXIII.

I'M EVERMORE KISSING HER IN THE AIR.

HE laughing sun had pushed the snow off the mountain, and warm zephyrs had fanned from the scene wintry airs, and spread it with tissued mantles of grasses, buds, and flowers, when our mine refused to yield any more golden grains. Its crevices, that hitherto had opened lips to show us mouthfuls of nuggets, were now gemless, and we wandered through the echoing rifts and gorges prospecting for new deposits.

Tom became intolerable. He would go to the shady side of the thickets, and stretch himself upon the soft sward, crushing down a broad swath of wild flowers, and with a stone for a pillow—rather two stones, for he took two, putting the smaller ends together, forming a hollow in the middle for his head—dream away the bright days. There he would lie motionless, fat, strong, personified health; awake, yet asleep to every thing about him. Or he would take his pick and pan into the shadows of the bluffs among which we prospected, and sit upon a mossy bowlder with about a hundred of Leina's old letters on the moss at his feet, and read them. He did not read them with any method, not consecutively as to dates, too much trouble to sort 'em; but as his hand happened to clutch one from the pile he read it, turned back, read it again, and re-read it, sitting still, in one posture, like a ruddy, long-whiskered, pensive, puffed corpse. It did not occur to me at first what ailed him. I knew he was at times subject to fits of—laziness. So for a week or two I said nothing remindful of his career. But it grew worse and worse. He neither dug in the pits, nor cooked, nor brought wood nor water, nor kindled fires, nor set nor cleaned the table— log rather—nor washed dishes; but he ate. However, about the tenth day of this rôle his appetite failed some, except when Mack killed a deer; and might have failed much more without specially diminishing the toils of his gastric juices, to whose thorough exercise he ever deemed it venial to devote much time and care. He grumbled more than a farmer. And a farmer—peace and plenty to him!—grumbles at rain and dry, sun, moon, stars, day, night, cloud, clear, hay, barley, wheat, flocks, herds, oats, corn, cotton, earth, weather, and nothing, year in and year out. In this Tom was already, what he thought himself to be in every thing prospectively, a model farmer—though of farming he knew nothing; he grumbled at every thing. The trees, though full of leaves, were leafless and cast no thick shades; the water, though the best, was brackish. The cheery skies were dismal, the hills of beauty were hideous. The graceful birds and their songs were unmusical, pestiferous little imps. The flowers were ugly, their odors poisonous, though of odor they were devoid. And every one and every thing were obnoxious, outrageous.

So I went to one of his trysting-places one day, and said: "Tom, you are going to die."

"I know it," he replied; "I have been feeling it coming on me a long time, ever since Pike left us. I am going to get out of this miserable, sickly, sterile, heathen, hateful country soon, if I have strength enough left, and die among civilized beings and objects. If I ever get away from it, I'll never come to it again till eternity wraps it in flames. And, Quien, you had best leave, too. I've been telling Virginia and Mack, the last month, that you are looking pale, thin, like a bloodless skeleton, like a castaway mariner bound to a rock to starve by a thousand miles of waves. You have fallen off nearly as much as I have; and I'm so weak I can scarcely walk, much less work. It hurts me to talk; something's the matter with my lungs; my breath is short." And falling over upon his back in a thicker part of the shade, he groaned, and made out by dint of exertion to put his giant-like wrist in my hand, and said: "Examine, please, and tell me what is the matter with me."

I felt his pulse, laid bare his broad, fat breast, thumped it heavily with the sharp points of my knuckles, put my ear on his solid chest to listen to the regular rhythm of his perfect lungs, felt his steely muscles, had him put out his tongue as far as he could get it—scraped it with his bowie-knife, and looked down his sound throat, tickling its palate and glands with a grassy spray till he had several paroxysms of coughing, made him spread his feet wide apart as possible, and looked at him.

He watched me mournfully the while; and as my face hardened and grew sad, his became gloomier, and he said with betwixt-a-sigh-and-sob tone, "Well!"

"Well," I replied, "the case is unmistakable. How long have you been so?"

"I think it struck me," he said, "about last Christmas. But what is it? Is it fatal?"

"The malady," I replied, "is like Clay's baby's whitening—a natural one. It is deeply seated, *fearful* in your case; the deadly fit is on you now."

"In the name of Leina, Quien," he said, "and all that's good, tell me what it is, and how long I can last."

"It's an attack," I replied, "of incomparable laziness and befuddled nostalgia."

Springing to his feet, he muttered the word "fool," and walked away rapidly toward the mountain, and we saw him scale a monster rock, with the agility and strength of a grizzly, and disappear in the *shady* dell beyond.

That night he said to me: "You are right. I am homesick unendurably. Leina is ever before me; I'm evermore kissing her in the air, and talking to her. The children are constantly climbing into my lap, upon my shoulders, or yelling delightedly about me. 1 see them all, awake or asleep. I know they are weary of boarding. Leina always insisted that a family is never so happy as when in a home of its own. One's own house, trees and grass, and flower-plats, one's own folks and birds within and without doors, one's own home is a heart-garden though a wilderness is its bower, a waste its outlook, and poverty its purveyor. I settled it on the mountain to-day. I am going to Leina. I have been figuring it up; I have sent to her the last few years not quite twenty thousand dollars;" like all his figuring, wrong, and this time by as much again in his favor; "it's little enough to begin farming with on *my* plan. But I'll soon quadruple it. Mack and Virginia and you must share the gold now in hand, if you'll pay my fare home; for I have been a dead-head a long time."

And home he started the next day with barely nuggets enough to ticket him through. But a check for nearly seven thousand dollars, his share of the gold in hand when he left, danced over the billows for him, without his knowledge, in the same steamer that bore him from the golden State.

CHAPTER XIV.

DARK-EYED SEÑORITAS WAITING THEIR COMING.
THE DEAD ONE IN THE HEART OF THE FLAMES.

HE rigor and toil, mining in wet pits, had made it judicious for Virginia to take a valley vacation. He left, with his pack upon his back, for a trading-post; thence he journeyed mule-back. He returned within the month healthy as ever, with stories of fresh cream and milk, and butter, and grapes, and honey, and peaches, and women and children, so delightful to us in the telling that we knew he had dipped in the borders, at least, of conventional life again, and regretted that we had not shared the trip. But we had uncapped a paying placer just before he got back, which contented us.

We had learned to value him specially for the information, trustfulness, and quiet courage that were transparent in his clear-cut character. The good manners that obtain in the unpretentious class of cultured Virginians graced him habitually. I have often thought that the reason why the Mexican had not killed him before he neared our camp the night of the snow-storm, was because he feared to make alone, even an assassinous stroke against him, and wished to get him to his brother's camp where help would be at hand. But fearing he could not decoy him farther, he took the chances with the precipice to help him to murder him, at a blow and the fall, with nothing to betray him. But the belt of gold prevented, and the surprised scream revealed him. So he took neither life nor gold. Virginia had remarked concerning it: "He could have slain me anywhere along the route, for not a suspicion of evil in him had crossed my mind."

The valley trip had its strange scenes, too, for Virginia. But we must let you hear *him* tell them in the tent-door with us.

"We moved along," he said, "man and mule snuffing the breeze spiced with the fragrance of clover and wild grasses, to the Merced valley. The trail wound south of the beaten track, across bald hills, one and another with mural sides, and through valleys pent into little plats, and a gray streak of dust marked the gravelly track we made across the plains. I got to a bluff of the willowy river about noon one day, and leaving the mule to feed in grass breast-high to him, I noted, while lunching, the valley scene. It was about three miles from bluff to bluff at that place, and widened to the view down the narrow river that looked in its rocky channel like flowing silver. A mile below me an isle-like hill, shaded with broad oaks, lifted its bust above the willows and vines; and lakes of clover around it in which cattle appeared to be swimming and browsing as in green waves. And herds and flocks fed also upon and around it, looking like elephants in the mirage that magnified them, as they moved from plat to plat, or stood upon the isle-top and looked down upon the green stretches, and the seemingly swimming pine. The bees drumming about me from flower to flower, and the quaint speckled magpies in the cosy nooks with their fussy courtesies, kept me company till the cool of the evening, when I set out down the valley to find a ranch. Regiments of crows were in flight over it, and here and there a cawing straggler skirred by to overtake the main body. Now and then a deer bounded away from the lonely pitapat of my mule along the trail, and sped toward the plains. Fawn-like rabbits loped carelessly about me, and the whir of an eagle quickened my pulse, as he bore one of them squeaking into the willows. A bear, at the edge of a blackberry thicket, reared on his haunches and held out his arms to greet me. And twilight came, and darkness settled upon the valley, and yet I had found no ranch. The rank weeds interwove across the untraveled trail, as throngs of fire-flies lit up the path for me with their dancing candles. A wolf howled near me, and the querulous coyotes screamed their peculiar chorus. I had begun to feel nervous enough, when a fierce growl a few yards to my left, scared my mule from under me, or me off my mule. At any rate I found myself, quicker than I can tell it, on my back in the weeds, and then on a limb up an old oak, whose outstretched boughs tangled, may be, at the affrighted leap I made to get into them. I listened, from the limb, to my mule plunging frantically through a lagoon, as he tore away across the gloomy bottom. But a nearer trouble claimed my thought, a noise like dogs craunching bones; and I could see dimly the willows sway to and fro in that particular spot. Just then other fierce growls woke up my hair, and soon the pack of wolves snapped and howled, fighting round my tree, as though the bone of contention trembled about where I sat on the limb. In a few minutes, however, some had trotted back to the thicket, though several remained at the foot of the tree munching the hard-worn fragments.

"The timber of the valley has one defect; occasionally a ponderous limb, shooting out at right angles from the body of the tree thirty or forty feet, by weight of foliage and action of heat and dry winds, would snap asunder suddenly and crash to the ground. This had not occurred to me perched in my leafy retreat, but soon the reminder came. For as I was safely, as I thought, peering down to fix the number and position of the wolves, a sudden pop-pop, and my limb crashed to the ground. I clutched for my knife as I fell, and yelled with horror. Though tangled in the branches of the fallen limb, and struggling to swing myself into another bough, I was aware by the "oughs" of the wolves, and the thuds of their wild leaps as they fled from the place, that they thought something had happened—what, they should n't stay to see. But neither did I stop for any thing till I was secure in the topmost fork of the tree. I discovered, up there, that in my fright I had not even drawn my knife from its sheath. So if the wolves

had attacked and had not fled, I should have
been as easy a prey as the deer whose fragments they were gnawing when I dropped
among them. They, doubtless, were terrified
by my yell, for there is truth in the saying
that the beasts of the forests are frightened at
the human voice. My downfall taught me how
to quicken a dull mind; for the velocity with
which mine traced my body into pieces, and
each piece turned into a wolf, was quick as a
wink, had seen it all before the first pop of the
breaking limb had more than touched the alert
ear. But as the night wore on, and the merry
stars slyly winked at me, my mind dipped into
the sea of laughing ether till the tree-top itself ,
seemed happy with merriment.

"Soon the moon rose and poured pale glory
upon every thing, yet her light revealed to my
eager eye no sign of human habitation. And
now the ticking of my watch was the noisiest
sound I heard for an hour, except the cry of
an owl, that seemed too lonesome to hoot more
than once; for a few moments after its mournful call died out it sailed on silent wing over
my retreat, and I watched it out of sight moving up the winding river. The flight of the
old necromancer deepened my sense of dreari-
ness, yet reminded me of the convenience of

my leafy observatory for a talk with the stars. But to every thing I said to them they replied by only widening their bright eyes, and in jerky fidgets; and I lamented that I had no magic to entice them to tell me of the worlds they journeyed around, the strange spaces they traversed, their sufferings and their joys. .

"That wonder, midnight, lay dreaming; dreaming in the firmament, dreaming on groves and river and plain. The shadows under the trees, the moonbeams in the air, were asleep. Nature had folded her starry mantle around her, and, leaning on the arm of God, breathed softly in trustful slumber. And incessant chant, drawn from the harp of solitude, in noiseless gush poured through the brain its mysterious delirium, thrilling the being with harmonies, till in its witchery the soul is conscious that not a sound in earth's realm rivals the musical reverie then dreamed by the ear. What is it?

"Is it the rhythmic voices of light coming, ever coming adown the heavens, to mingle with the voices of the blood gurgling out of the 'golden bowl,' flowing ever in softest strains, to cheer the body as it wears away?

"From the sky it floats down, from the earth it floats up, inaudible, yet well heard, the voice-

less music of silence. We *see* the silent flow
of the wave when the air lies asleep upon its
crest, but we *feel* the liquid sound thereof.
The melody of silence is articulate like it.

"Is it the music of the spheres? Can we
catch it, retain it long enough to word one
sweet strain of its countless euphonies? Here
they are above, beneath, around, within us,
softly opening every fountain of the soul till
it smiles, or weeps, or shouts a voiceless shout
of joy, and feels like leaping out upon the sea
of space to melt away and float off with the
silent strains that come, always come pouring
through us into the heart the melodies of silence.

"Is it the song of the sun-rays dying in the
lap of night? Or is it the gushing up to the
ear of God of the secret prayers of the good of
earth, meeting the answers coming down from
the throne of grace?

"The little children in their white robes,
ready for crib and trundle, kneeling, hands
clasped, hearts reverencing, lips parted, prat-
tling tongues naming to God Jesus. What
a little mighty company! What a cloud of
prayers of innocence toddling up through the
solitude of space! How low and musical their
voices! What sweetness must their echoes
trace upon each airy wavelet that lies between

their little naked knees and the throned Christ
sending by cherubim the smiles of God down
upon them. This music of silence, is it the
echoes of child-voices? saying:

> Now I lay me down to sleep,
> I pray thee, Lord, my soul to keep;
> If I should die before I wake
> I pray thee, Lord, my soul to take, ·
> For Jesus' sake. Amen.

"I know not what it is. I know that it is;
that it voices somehow to the soul a mysterious
melody that sets it to thinking of 'the things
unseen.'"

Mack interrupted him here. His practical
mind seemed to take alarm at "the melodies
of silence," and he suggested: "Is not silence
comparative, not absolute. Can there be a
moment when there are not sounds in nature?
and if a sound, her silence is not complete;
and the waves of sound bearing a sound, however soft and low, disturb sources of sound
that add another voice, and these others as they
swim in the spaces; and so the noiseless solitude is really vocal with sounds so tender, it
may be, that the ear cannot articulate them,
separately, from the music of the blood forever
flowing in its mechanism.

"Thought may have a sound that reports it

to thought; mercy may have a song as she comes with blessing; emotion may have notes that make its presence felt, but so soft that the ear cannot hold them longer than only for the soul to catch them, yet not to note their artic- ulation. In a world of sound-forces, many of them must be ringing every moment, and their journeying cadences refined, etherealized, min- gling with the blood's song in the ear, are the melodies of silence. We hear them in, they sound in, silence in that from its quiet realm every harsher note is excluded. Your tree-top reverie of melody must have been delightful."

"Yes," replied Virginia, "it was; and the fact deepened my regret when I saw, before I heard them, two horsemen, one close after the other, coming straight across the bottom. The pale moonbeams revealed their girdles of weapons. The jingle of their heavy spurs, and the grating of the horses' hoofs crossing a rocky lagoon, frighted from the willows a band of antelope that fled in pell-mell leaps under my tree, passing toward the southern bluffs. They came on leisurely as before, however, those dusky midnight riders, as though not a pulse were quickened by the sky-lit bounds of the brown racers. They rode with bowed heads, only every few rods they turned them quickly right and left, peering athwart the waste, and reined up in a group of trees within a hundred feet of me.

"Striking a match they lit cigarettes, which, when puffed into thin smoke that drooped in the breathless quiet, they replaced with others. And without having exchanged a syllable, they moved into the thickets of willows; and in a little while the waters splashed over there as they crossed the river going toward Tulare. I had felt for my purse on sight of them, but it was already gone. Before they came I had sighed for the presence of man, and scanned the dreary bottom again and again, hoping to glimpse a human being. But the long breath I drew when they were out of sight, out of hearing, left me contented to be alone. Whither were they going, on what errand, to what fate, those speechless, nighted, heavily armed, gloomy Mexicans?

"Perhaps they were edging ruin that soft night of witchery; and on their souls the shadows had fallen, like ghosts tokening to them the hurrying woe. Perhaps they were 'honest miners' tired of the gold-hunt, and were speeding to the banana-groves of their tropic homes, dreaming, as they went, of the dark-eyed señoritas waiting, watching, yearning for their coming. God keep them in the way if they had pure love in their hearts! For the angel Love works no ill to his neighbor. A lineal descendant of the skies, heaven lives where he dwells, and blesses where he lives. When upon a world of hate Jesus looked, he wept, and laying a hand of blessing on it, said, 'Love.'"

"Mexicans," said Mack, "love señoritas with romantic flames, but experience little of its thrill toward Anglo-Americans. They are bitter, and I do not say unjustly so, that we have overlapped their golden borders. Yet Mexico, a mine of gems, an agricultural alluvium, a pastoral, foliaged with precious stones, fruits, and flowers, is kindling for fusion with us. Its legends of tribal glory, its romances of love and gold and power, the glitter of its semi-barbarous religion, like the aisles of a cathedral in ruins thronged with precious memories, are dear to its people. Yet they are aspiring to the surpassing realities that base and zone and canopy our Protestant realm with order, liberty, and prosperity."

"Their destiny," said Virginia, "shall, I hope, be as glorious as their land. But the tree-top in the valley was more peaceful by far to me when the Mexican horsemen were gone.

And, as if rejoicing with me, several meteors traced bright paths through the sea of air, and I joyfully observed their spangled trails fade from purple into hazy blue, and perish in the horizon. Sleep's lethed sensations were steeping me with forgetfulness afterward, when a bright light eclipsed the stars, accompanied by a muffled roar, and the burning meteor, several inches in diameter, raced athwart the heavens, and far out over the western plains burst into fragments, and in hundreds of sparkles dropped out of sight.

"Over me the planets had shone all night, and poured steady glory on the scene, and I honored them with quiet glances only. But this glary, fussy thing had lifted me to my feet in the tree-top, and won by its red rush my admiration and wonder. It was the creature of a moment, of eccentric course, without brave steadiness of flames; had suddenly burst out its soft brains against the pure ether it essayed to voyage, while the planets, from their lofty heights were still shining, forever shining steady, constant, true. And I said: 'I am what Tom called Quien in the trysting-place diagnosis—a fool; the nearest wonder charms me most.' But I sat down again in my aerie, though delighted still with my meteor; and comfort, that sometimes comes from very unseemly sources, came to me in the thought that I was not an uncommon fool at any rate. For the meteor is only the demagogue among the stars, hazing their splendors by its skylarking flight and hum. And is it not common to applaud the demagogue? He rolls in meteoric glare between us and the true, great men, and we laud his gyratory career, neglectful of the modest, unselfish, real, great workers in Church and State, who flood the world with good.

"The meteor had repelled the tides of sleep, and its short life and tragic death evoked memories almost smothered by the cumulose experiences of the gold-fields. Of these memories, 'school-days' were just then freshest; and the boys of long ago rose up like visions of hope, and grew larger as they came toward the tree, and at its roots they were men; and one and another came climbing up to me in a jolly way, till many were there with me, grouped about upon the limbs. Soon a change came over them from merry to serious, till the tree appeared to be peopled by men with folded arms, reflecting upon all the way their feet had come in the journey of life. They represented the professions, and several industrial arts.

Some had achieved distinction, most were hopefully biding it. There were others whose happy voices rang in memory's play-ground, who grouped not with us now, but were sleeping in graves among pines and palms and oaks. Some fell in the red fields of the Mexican war; several perished in personal feuds; over others fevers had piled the earth; delirium tremens had raged away the lives of two or three; others were dead though living, for licentiousness had made them loafers. Yet even these lazily sauntered to the tree, and sung out in the old time tones, 'Halloo, boys! come down out o' that!'

"You have met an hour that brought about you the boys, and their traits, you were a boy with, now grown to be men; and of them there was not one that you did not feel, however life had muddied him, like putting your arms around, and talking over with him the scrapes and joys you and he had shared together. Such an hour was this to me; and though I knew not if one of them was on the coast, yet here they were with me, treed; even the ghosts of some seemed to be sitting about among the living; now a rolicking company, now a moody though cheerful older company, dearer for the lines of care, dearer for the casts of thought the conflicts of years had printed on their brows. How the old heart, manhood's heart, goes back, backward, backward, arms stretched out, to rub against its play-day mates, and turns when it touches them, to greet them with smiles and words as in the long ago. So I mused till, when I looked about me again, my old playmates were all gone. They had dropped out of the tree one after another, while I was thinking, and hid from me. I called, and they would n't answer, and I scringed lest some mischievous ones of them were about to 'chunk' me out the tree-top from their hiding-places. But they were gone, the happy hour that bore them to me would not be recalled. Pike seemed then to stretch himself on the big limb next me, and leaning on his elbow with his old self-poise, said to me, as he did in our last hunt together: 'Virginny, as our old mates drop from the path o' the living, and vanish out o' sight, so some time it will be with us. Do n't forget, Virginny, to be ready for that time.' And he had gone, too, and I was alone again among the tenantless boughs.

"The short night was verging toward morning when a fire sprung up in the solitary bottom a few hundred yards back of me. It was a full blaze when I first beheld it, and the nearly naked forms of many Indians were soon mov-

. ing about it. Their grotesque shapes were sharply defined as they passed between me and the fire they had kindled in a heap of dry logs. And I saw, as a band of them placed upon the pyre the dead body of one of the tribe, that many others hurried to pile upon the glowing heap great fragments of dry drift-wood. They reminded me of fiends tottering under burdens of fuel to add to perdition's fury. Soon their dead comrade was ablaze, and his limbs, as the burning heap jostled and settled, moved and twisted about, and the whole form afire seemed to writhe in convulsions, as the flames moved this way and that, as the startled air rushed from or toward the pyre. The black smoke went up in gusts, and hung in dark clouds just above them, and every now and then the red heat and dancing sparkles shot up, in fantastic gyrations, into its bosom, then dropped back to the crackling heap whose hissing roar drummed in my ear. The Indians had formed in bands a few yards from the pyre, and now and then gestured; and I caught the notes of a wild chant. Soon they whirled in frenzied circles round and round the burning mass; and moans and shrieks reached me, resounded like some imp-ish dirge breaking upon the chaste wastes of

14

paradise. Round and round and around they whirled in leaping, capering antics; distorting, contorting their dark, squirmy bodies; now solemnly erect, then rushing in frantic coils round the burning pyre again and again, until they seemed to be the black, impish, quivering brink of h—l. Then they fell apart, down, and rolled over and over without the fire circle, into the shadow of the trees, and uttered a woful howl that agonized through the grove, and shattered into fiercely mournful echoes against the thicker belt of timber that bordered the river. Then all was silence, not an Indian in sight but the remnants of the dead one in the heart of the flames. Suddenly an old gray-haired man, and crone, hopped out from the shadow into the circle of light, and crouched together close to the smoldering body. They were still as stumps, save every now and then they lifted their hands on high and wrung them; and I knew they were chanting a wail, as sounds like sorrow tortured once or twice filled me with a pathetic grief I could not re-sist, until their lorn stark scream shrieked through the tree-top where I sat, startling me to my shivering feet, as they tossed over and over back into the shadows again.

"Presently other fires were kindled, and the

squaws were engaged in toasting pieces of flesh and entrails of beasts, and bearing them on scales of bark to the warriors squatting on the sward. And I saw one snatch a raw entrail from the clutch of a squaw, and eat it dangling between his teeth, with a greedy gusto like a beast. Soon several dusky runners entered upon the scene bearing the black bottles of civilization, and the whisky gave to the execrable feast a turn that made the camp appear like the habitation of dragons.

"How beautiful to me then was Christianity! The burial scene, long ago, of my little winsome, soft-eyed sister passed before me. The tasteful temple, the delicate case covered in flowers, the prayers and hopeful words of the minister, and sweet hymns of the decorous assembly, the words of the resurrection shedding light upon the flowered grave where we left her asleep in Jesus, were to me a charm like voices from the heavenly world."

We were silent now. For involuntary tears had fallen along Virginia's cheeks, from the moment he had said "my little winsome, soft-eyed sister," and his words thenceforward had been tremulous and low and tender, till he paused. And I must trust you to pardon me for saying that I stepped without the tent into the shadows; for my little sister Addie, too, had said to me when she died: "I shall be in heaven, brother, waiting, just waiting to kiss you there, Quien." And she seemed to me to be saying the words to me again, in her coaxing, soft way, and I did not care to be seen weeping. O there are words niched away in the heart's depths that touch it so tenderly, at times, that it would nearly break were it not for tears!

CHAPTER XXV.

HER EYES WAS MIGHTY STRETCHT, AN' SCART-LIKE.

Y dawn," said Virginia, when he resumed his narrative, "the Indians were gone; and descending from the tree, I found my purse among the branches of the limb that had fallen with me early in the night. I pursued the mule's track, and wading the lagoon, found my blanket pack just beyond it. After going three or four miles I met an Iowan who told me he had corralled the mule, and was tracing its tracks to discover the rider. 'I am glad,' he said, 'that you are safe, and within a mile can welcome you to a breakfast of salmon and flapjacks.' He added, as we moved toward his ranch: 'Let me persuade you to tarry with me a spell. Just now is a time of leisure with me; stay, and help me to be lazy.' The proposal being 'pat to my natur',' as Pike used to intimate, I accepted, thanking him for discerning my talent.

"'Your talent,' he said, 'is not rare. I devoted yesterday to the lazy problem; and calc'-lating 1,200,000,000 people in the world, I fig-ured up seven industrious members of the small community; and the laziness of the re-mainder averaged twenty tons each. I put you down at fifty tons.'

"'Me!' I exclaimed; 'you knew nothing of me. How did you manage to particularize so nicely?'

"'A month or so ago,' he replied, 'I traveled by stage with a ruddy man who described his claim, and said he could have gotten rich upon it were it not for three of his partners, who, besides being the poorest of financiers, were the most industrious miners at being lazy in the gold-fields, and that one of them would visit this valley this season. That's the way I come at the heft of you talent. I take you to be one of Rothleit's partners.'

"Our pleasantest and a novel amusement was shooting salmon as they struggled up the shallows of the river, or were resting in the crystal pools. They were easily killed by rifle, or revolver, as far below the surface as six to eight inches; but to obtain them certainly, after having shot them, it was important that the bullet pierced their heads just back of the eyes; then they invariably floated to the surface with faint struggles, and were pulled ashore with canes, or taken as they floated down the shallows. We lost several seven or eight pounders by inaccurate shots; and when any were missed, it was strangely exciting to observe their alarm at the concussion, and the agile freaks of curves and angles they displayed in darting to shelter in the clear depths.

"The Indians capture them with a long stick, to one end of which a nail or piece of hard wood is bound so as to dangle, to which a string is attached that tightened along the pole brings the nail to a point when thrust into the fish, but falls to a horizontal when the string is loosed; and the lithe creature cannot then get away, however it struggles, unless an opening tear through its sides two or three inches long. With this instrument they take many of them in the running season. They follow the river for miles, the squaws carrying their infants upon their backs in funnel-shaped baskets, or willow lathes, and piles of salmon also; for their haughty lords scout every burden, except consummate ugliness be one.

"While wandering on the river-side, I saw a company of them catching small fish. They dived to the bottom, and felt with their hands under the roots and rocks and banks; and often they would bound to the surface, a fish between their teeth, and one in each hand. Occasionally they posed, as they rose to the surface, with a cunning leer at their sweethearts on the shore, as though about to eat. alive the wriggling fish between their teeth, and *their* darlings looked down upon them, and smiled. So the Indian, though his life is dark with savagery, has his Red Cloud to gild it with joy.

"Everywhere, woman is the earth-angel. In this instance her black hair is coarse as horsemane, grows low down upon her forehead, is quite unkempt; but it is her own, not borrowed; *hair*, not flossed bark. This she leaves to the Blonde Cloud who pours smiles upon the Indian's kind—Christianized white brother, who never cheats him of any of his land except the whole of it, nor of any of his fisheries and game-haunts except all of them.

"Wearying of fish, we crossed the treeless plains southward to visit an old Arkansas frontiersman whose life had been spent trapping and hunting. We soon parted in the roll of hills, attempting to reach different bands of antelopes, and I had ridden an hour without more than glimpsing him upon the brown landscape. While watching a band of antelopes grazing, at the base of a knoll, in the manner of goats, he turned the point at full speed and gave chase to the surprised, bounding creatures, singling from the rest a lordly stag, whose dingy antlers like sprangled stalactites were thrown back on its shoulders as it sped wildly toward the tules. The space slowly diminished between them till, ere eight hundred yards had been raced, white puffs of smoke told me the revolver was at work, and in a few more convulsive leaps the antlered king fell over upon the sward, his last race run; and we left him there upon his native heather. The Iowan said: 'This is the second antelope I have fairly outrun with this mustang. A really fleet horse would have come up with him in two-thirds the distance. Antelopes scarcely ever go more than a mile in three minutes.'

"The mustang, as to beauty of form, speed, and bottom, is usually overstated. The domesticated horse often excels him in those qualities, as well as in docility. He is too, perhaps invariably, tricky to the end. The one my friend rode was a select specimen, and had been subdued to the saddle for three years. Yet I would not have risked his bucking deviltry—or, to phrase it less aptly, bucking ingenuity—for him. His master, however, seemed to grow to him joyfully in his mad, stiff-legged, bouncing, jerking leaps, to unseat him, of which *'bucking'* is the descriptive appellation.

"The flowers had retreated from the plains to the quaggy spots of the valley, and fringed them with variegated beauty. And the wild oats, having long matured, had fallen before the winds and wild animals, and were lying in tangles of waste over thousands of smooth acres. The old hunter had pitched his tent near the bank of the small river of the valley we had entered. Perhaps the name, Mariposas Butterflies, was given expressive of its flowery splendor in spring attracting myriads of that many-hued insect, to wing away their short lives, dancing through its charming mazes.

"He was absent, but his wife and children welcomed us. Our meal was stewed rabbit and boiled cracked wheat—nothing else, save the inimitable pleasantry of the apologies of the hostess. What a being is an amiable, pure-spirited woman! That dinner was a luxury, made so by the welcome of the heart, which set a joy with us richer than a feast at which no viands were missing, not even a welcome but this lacking the unique grace of expression and manner of this daughter of the frontier. She knew nothing of 'polite life,' yet so truly did she blend in her character the high virtues of refined womanhood that a princess could not have exceeded her in commanding respect and imparting happiness.

"But the hunter was at home an hour after dinner with supplies, and made us know we were as near home as we could be outside our own tents. We were on the plains next morning, and by midday had killed more antelopes than we could conveniently pack to the tent. We had lunched and napped upon the carpet of clover, under some low-boughed oaks, when our eyes were arrested by a far-off rifleman afoot, passing toward the valley. And the hunter's spy-glass brought his form so near that he recognized him as his brother; and the Iowan rode briskly away, leading a horse to bear him to our shade. He ate the remainder of our lunch while detailing a murder perpetrated thirty miles away two nights before. He said: 'It was jest two old folk a-livin' by therselves; an' they lived in as pritty a cove as runs out from the main valley of the Merced, a leetle way among the hills. They was as innercent a good old couple as you ever see, a-tryin' to be happy by hard work, an' nobody lived nigh onto them. A caravan o' Mexicans had spent the day close by, and had bought melons from 'em. They went to bed arly, and a leetle arter night set in some Mexicans come in their tent and cut the poor old man to death, an' tied the ole 'oman an' rolled her under the bed onto the dirt floor, an' tol' her one on 'em would stay thar and watch her ontil mornin', an' ef she moved he would cut her heart out alive. An' thar she lay ontil arter midnight, poor ole fursaken creetur, a-scart to ketch her breath a'most; the blood out o' her husband's heart were a-drappen' off the bed onto her face, an' all about on her. But hearin' nothin' but the blood draps a-patterin' agin her cheeks an' 'bout on her hands an' dress, an' the owls a-hooten' in the tree over the tent, she arter awhile ontied herself, an' peered 'bout in the dark, for the moon wern't nigh riz, an' the blessed ole creetur as she crept about slipped down in the blood an' hurt herself. But seein' an' hearin' nothin', she crept out into the dark, an' crossed the river, an' the bar thickets, an' the big bottom 'mong the beasts, ontil she got out on t'other side, an' went to the stage-stand afore day-break, an' tole 'em thar about it. Her eyes was mighty stretcht, an' still, an' scart-like, when she were a-talkin' o' the blood a-drippin' an' a-fallin' pitapat, drip, drip, pitapat, pit, pit, pitapat on her face an' neck; an' like the tarnal fool I allus was, I went to cryin' an' a-breshin' the blood off o' her, a-sayin': 'Never you mind it any more, mother; never you mind it; you 's 'mong frien's *now*. We 'll captivate 'em afore noon, an' regerlate 'em by ther necks to a limb.' But the women tuck her right away to ther room, an' was a-whisperin', an' runnin' round mighty soft in no time; fur they said she were fainted.'

"We were all silent before the naked horror of the statement. And the hunter's brother added: 'We sarched the valley and the hills for them murderin' robbers, but found none we could believe was the right ones.'

"'I have read,' said the Iowan, making a slight rift in the gloom the story had put upon us, 'that the man who commits one homicide is likely to kill others; that to shed blood creates an inclination to shed blood.'

"'I have learned to b'lieve *that*,' replied the hunter; 'I 've known it to be that way. A human is like a miser'ble lion that 's got a taste o' our blood—he 's greedy to lap it ag'in. Better destroy a man-killer afore he kills someboby else; he 's whetted up fur it. It 's so with me. I hate a snaky Injun wherever I sees him, an' am real sorry these pesky Cali-

forny tribes ain't wuth shootin'. I've had so
many fracases with ther sort on the branches
o' the Massysip that my fingers naterly feel
for the trigger when I see one o' the yallar
sarpints. I feel like shootin' him just to see
him jump, or to hear his death-yell at the
crack o' the gun. I've got at my tent now the
best razor-strap you ever see, made out'n a
piece o' the hide o' one on 'em we killed atween
Pike's Peak an' the Platte. I'll show it to you
when we get back thar to-night.'

"And dreading lest there might be truth in
his theory, I said to him on the spot: 'Friend,
I'm black-haired, and rather dark, sun-tanned,
you know; and my clothes are none of the best.
If you see an Indian on the plains this evening, take second look before you shoot; may
be it's me. And I'm not ready yet for the
jump and death-yell at the crack of your gun.'

"That night at the tent he showed us his
'Injun-hide razor-strap,' and it was a good
one. It was thick as calf-skin, open-grained,
yet delicately smooth to the touch. And he
said, 'I stripped it off from atween his
shoulders.'"

CHAPTER XXVI.

APPEARED AS THOUGH THE DEAD WERE RISEN,
AND WERE MOVING, GROUPING, PARTING IN
NOISELESS AWE.

OCALITIES affect us. Mountains impart their ruggedness, not rudeness; valleys their softness. In the one the mind dreams quick, clear, but dreams, yet mounts over obstructions, adhering to its purpose till the height is attained. It then rests up there and drinks in the scenes above, about, below, and throws back to the strugglers up an exhilarant call, and bends over the brink to give a firm helping hand to them, who, clinging among the crags, have a few more crevices to thrust fingers and toes in carefully, *well as they can*, holding on, straining up, to get on top to do likewise.

In the other, the mind dreams, dreams softly; wanders along and wanders; and in the quietness and restfulness of the scenes, it takes in the soft sweet thoughts of life, and dallies

with them, fondles them till it becomes enam-
ored with the nicer delights of the heart and
leaps all separating distances and floats over
every barrier, and counts all else but loss, till
it embraces and is caressed by them. At least,
so it had been with Tom. In the mountains,
among their jumbled heights, jutting promon-
tories, and wild chasms, he was a jubilate, keeping, however tired as he always was, joyfully
to his one purpose of gold. But soon as he
snuffed the valleys, and dwelt among the little
hills that bordered them, the tender things of
life asserted themselves till, as he said, he was
forever kissing them in the air. And so it was
now with Virginia: his return from the valley
was the signal of his return to the Atlantic
States. For, as we were sitting one day in early
autumn among the laughing hills, he said:
"I shall leave by the next steamer for the
Atlantic States; shall go to Kentucky first after landing in New York."

I was not at all surprised when he said
"Kentucky first," for when he said it he had
open in his palm the locket that contained the
little bright, quiet picture he had shown to
us in the snow-storm among the peaks. So
we sold the claim, divided gains, saw him
aboard ship at San Francisco, and went again

into the Sierras far northward, and took into partnership an experienced miner called "Maine."

Though we discovered a rich placer among rollicking cascades and echoing forests in the depths of the mountains, the new environments somehow admitted to me hours of drearest depression. It must have been in one of the darkest of those evil hours that I wrote to Roth in New York, whither he had gone "to live forever," he said.

About that time insanity was busy with men's brains on the gold-fields. Dissipation, and hope wrecked, drifting to pieces like a holiday ship beaten to fragments by breakers on the reefs to the utter surprise of the gay voyagers, had lashed many minds into distraught fury, and set them raving on the gold-fields, or pursued them with blighted dreams to their old Atlantic homes, and smitten them there amid the soft, sweet scenes. Roth knew so much, or thought he did, at least he hoped so much, that I had often dreaded lest he should go daft. And at last the dread seemed to be fully realized; for, while visiting a town a dozen miles or more from the mine to get our mail, and deposit the gold we had accumulated, I received from him the following letter:

15

"Near C——, New York, ——.

"*Dear Quien:* Crazy. Gone mad. Insane. Been expecting it a long time. Go to the express-office. Come *here* at once. It will help me to see you. Leina's in much grief about it—in perfect sympathy with me. I am too nervous to write. In haste, yours,

"T. R. Rothleit."

After reading it I was strangely distressed about Roth—thought it specially hard that he had survived the gold-field mishaps to go crazy so soon after he got back safely to his family on the Atlantic slope. But I rejoiced that he had mind enough left to know that he was crazy, and to feel concern to have me with him in his drear paroxysms. So I consoled myself while retracing the trail athwart gorge and mount to the distant mine. Stepping from the zigzag trail a few yards, I rested on the skyed crag that hung over the pretty town. The town two thousand yards from me, and many feet below the crag, seemed, in the transparent atmosphere of the season, about to float up off the rocks and hills and ravines it occupied. Its streets appeared like mere alleys from the height, and the busy men appeared like small boys, and scarcely to move, though all astir, I knew; for it was "business hours," and they were on the rush. Ladies appearing like little girls, seemed not to walk but to float away from cottage gates, and pause as group met group, then drift apart and away so slowly that the mind was witched as the eye noted how they seemed to swim apart, standing in the ether, so softly and slowly that many moments elapsed before any separating space between them appeared to the beholder. Not a sound came up to the crag from the town; so they, men and women, appeared to me as though the dead were risen and were moving, grouping, greeting, parting, in noiseless awe. They moved apparently just above the ground, for their feet and lower limbs were indistinguishable, giving the impression that they were in a sea of ether, with those members under the surface; for not a footfall of all the many in view pressed the earth visibly to me.

As I gazed they were under sudden arrest, as if in the moment planted in the air where they stood. Up, down the streets they paused and faced in one direction. I saw two or three, quicker of will than the remainder, hurrying like little balloons in human shape, up a street whitherward every one seemed now to float— some faster, some slower, some veering about, some smoothly, but all floating, not running.

"Fire," I thought. But as the eye swept from point to point of, to me, the silent but really tumultuous town, no token of conflagration was seen. Soon the throngs poured together into and around a white cottage that crowned a hill like a smile of peace and hope; and I knew that *there* lay the motive whose electric spark had drawn them all to one spot. But I heard not the pistol-shot, nor saw from the crag nearer the sky the suicide in the rear of that pretty home, with the bullet in his brain, kneeling over on his face, who had thrilled the multitude with one thought—red-handed, hard, desperate death.

Now and then an incident grates upon the keel of our barques, journeying the sea of life, and fills us with dismay as chartless reefs do sailors on the deep. Such a one is when a sensitively honorable man, as in this instance, lays violent hands upon his own life and bursts through its casket into the presence of God. We inquire of the horror the cause, and only echo answers us; answers us whose eyes pierce not deeper than the reddened surface, whose ear hears only that which is voiced. But is it therefore hidden from retribution's inquest? And when this comes does it not often disclose that others' sins set aflame his heart with the evil fire of despair; that others, whom he had implicitly trusted, had beguiled him into a sea of trouble, and having stolen from him every refuge, left him to the tempestuous, reefy, chasmy waves, out of sight of rescue, to leap madly into the depths? They may survive— richer, mightier grow; yet how can *their* glory foil God—turn from them the arrows of his justice?

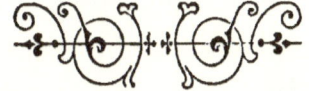

CHAPTER XXVII.

BONAPARTEAN.

N reaching the camp I said nothing to Mack about Roth's insanity; was averse to break to him the grewsome tidings of his old comrade and special friend.   He seemed, too, to be particularly reticent that night, and whenever I awoke he was sitting up, and threw quick, searching glances upon me. His voice had an anxious yet soothing tone when he spoke to me that was not its wont, for it was habitually an exhilarant voice that conveyed laughing gas.   He constantly faced me, too; was never at my side as aforetime; and in the morning I remarked that his pallet was untumbled.   If he slept at all during the night it was a nodding sleep from the camp-stool opposite me. He proposed that we should not mine that day, but rest and stroll, as he had brought on vertigo the day before by over-work.   It was ever an easy task, Roth always said, to persuade me not to work; so we lounged

away the slow, sunny hours till noon, when
Wyche L., Roth's cousin, came to us from
beyond a mountain eastward. He had come
a few years before, fresh from the college-
halls of New York, to California soon as he
had been graduated; had returned to his old
home, and was now back again on the gold-
fields. Skylarking is hardly descriptive of him,
but enough so to suggest the keenness with
which he discerned, enjoyed, and ministered to
the absurdities that everywhere in the gold-
fields bubbled to the surface. He and Mack
interviewed each other with a letter between
them, apart from me, after which I somehow
felt that they constantly and with kindly concern watched me. If I stepped to the mine to
have a word with Maine, who dug and scooped
and shoveled, visitors or no visitors, as though
he thought the gold was smothering to death
under the rocks, they followed me, noting
each movement and expression of face and
eyes. If I went to the spring, they kept me
in sight. If I entered the conversation, they
sadly glanced and blinked to each other the
while. So I scaled the mountain to see the
sun jostle his wheels against the coast-range
and plunge over into the sea out of sight; for
I tired of their surveillance. They were soon

at my side, with polite pleasantries as excuse for joining me.

It occurred to me that then was the opportune time to inform them that Roth had gone crazy; and I did so. Mack looked bewildered, and sadder by far than I had ever observed in him before; and Wyche appeared bewildered too, and strangely sobered. And I gave Roth's letter to Mack and asked him to read it out to us. After reading he dropped it on the ground, and his sorrowing eyes fell on my face and leaped to Wyche's in startled inquiry. Wyche was deeply dejected, and I began to regret having given them the tidings, when Wyche took a fit. He seemed to be in much pain—about to burst. He tossed about on the brown grass, bit his lips, pressed his sides with his hands, dug his heels in the turf, rolled over; his cheeks swelled; his eyes shone, twinkled, danced as they fell upon me; and he surrendered himself to the fit that convulsed him. We were in a few minutes about to bleed him with a small knife, but a wrenching spasm twitched him from between us, as his paroxysm whirled him to and fro in a boisterous wave of ridiculous laughter. But as he tossed to me the following letter Mack caught it away sadly as I was reaching for it, his kind face full of confusion.

" Nonsense, Mack, nonsense!" he exclaimed.
" He'll not mind Roth. They are both crazy.
Give him the letter."

And so he did, and here it is:

"———, NEW YORK, ——.

"*Dear Mack and Wyche:* I wish I were there
to help you with Quien S. I know you are
troubled to know what to do with him in his
insanity. You should have written to me about
it. I have only heard of it by a letter from
himself, and I infer from it that his chief de-
lusion—and many other evil delusions always
mix with that —is that he is haunted by an as-
sassin: a sick whim of his dazed intellect, of
course. While with him I had much ado
to keep him in his right mind, if he had
any such. He was my old partner, you know;
he can't help his brains, and I cannot but feel
very deep concern for him. Take the best care
of him for my sake.

"Usually you may do any thing with him
by kindness; but if this fails, and you are careful, you may readily scare him into meas-
ures. He has at times unwittingly helped me
out of trouble, and, somehow, I like him for
old toil's sake on your coast. Boys, stick to
him. Don't let him be taken to the lunatic
asylum at Stockton. I can cure him" (he had

but one cure for every ill—tincture of arnica). "Decoy him to the nearest town, and keep him in the best rooms of the hotel till one or both of you can start to New York with him by the November steamer. Spare neither yourselves nor money to make him comfortable. I'll foot all bills. Have remitted to him by express enough, I hope; ought to have directed it to Mack, who will please get it and use for Q." (Mack had got it.) "Don't chain him; bind him with *soft* ropes if he rages. Don't for the world hurt him. I would prefer to suffer half death than he should have a needless bruise.

"He nursed me when I had the small-pox, he called it; it was nothing but the nettle-rash, really, that developed under his treatment into a universal splotch of overgrown pimples, and pitted up my face a little" (it would have pitted him in a thousand spots but for me), "but it's all the same; he thought it was the small-pox. And, besides, I was about to be killed once, and he, accidentally no doubt, got mixed up in the melee, and trying to run out knocked over the man who was sticking his bowie into me, tripped one of the others who was pummeling me, and butted or got the other down somehow, so I easily managed the crowd. On some

other occasions he did me similar small favors.

"I would come for him myself, but Leina
dissuades me, and says 'she would make the
voyage for no such fool.' Boys, if you will be
kind to him, as you would to me in his condition, and bring him to New York yourselves, I
shall always thank you.

"Poor, simple-hearted fellow! He was trying to make money enough to return to the
States and marry—I forget whom; some sim-
pleton, doubtless. I suspect he has been chiseled out of every thing. He was never better
adapted to business than a Digger Indian is
to translate the Odes of Horace, or construe
the language and brain of Goethe, and is the
worst of financiers; hence his insanity.

"But I will meet you at the Astor House
1st of December. Yours, etc.,

"T. R. ROTHLEIT."

When I had read this letter, lying on the
turf propped upon my elbow, my right ear
clutched in my hand, Wyche had dismissed
the affair from his mind, but Mack still
watched for insane symptoms, evidently;
though he had never thought of one in me till
he had received the letter the day before, and
sent Wyche word to come to the mine. But

he at least repressed his doubts, and we returned the money to Roth with some exquisite specimens for his wife and children.

That night at the camp-fire California "church-going," among much else, was discussed, and Wyche said:

"Not long after I got to this country I attended a church service. The minister, in some illustrative paragraph, said: 'The First Napoleon was greatest of the Cæsars. Had he been like Washington, too great for a palace, too patriotic for a crown, his name could scarcely be peered on the roll of the ages. His genius mocked kings trampled thrones, and raised France to be a power so great as to require allied Europe in arms to repulse her. Nor was it till the monarchs knew that his ashes were urned in the rock in the ocean's heart that their crowns ceased to tremble.'

"A Frenchman rose to his feet, stepped into the aisle, paused a moment, marched to the pulpit, placed a coin from his thin purse upon the tablet, and fixing his eyes in the preacher's, said: 'Napole*yoon* le Grande! Frans*ay!* Napole*yoon!!* There, give you that; go now git you more. Napole*yoon!!!*'

"And the thrilled old Frank, leaving a Napoleon on the pulpit-tablet, marched down the aisle out of the church like a soldier of 'the old guard,' eyes flashing as though a volcano of Vives Napoleon were rumbling in his heart. I felt like the Fourth of July was present cheering the old Gaul, and was ready to' lock arms with him, and march down the aisle, America and France together.

"Some months after, I asked the preacher if he had met the Frenchman since. 'Yes,' he replied; 'as I stepped from the church to the sidewalk one Sunday afternoon, he was passing up the street by zigzags. On meeting me he paused, stood erectly, still as a statue a few moments, touched his cap in military salute style, and reeled on, his eye flaming as if he could leap through St. Helena. I intended, on opportunity, to return to him the coin, if it could be done with proper regard to his sensibilities; for I noticed at the time he gave it it was all his purse held, and I thought he was keeping it as a memorial of the France of his early years. But as he passed me, veering to and fro across the sidewalk like a ship lurching between waves, I knew it was no time for a nice parley. For then he had not only French fire in him (which may God bless), but hell-fire— that is, brandy—from which good Lord deliver us.' "

Mack, whose veins carried a strain of French, from his Creole mother, said:

"Napoleon's name will live wherever France has a son worthy her motherhood. It is magnetic. Here, with many years and continents and seas between him and France, a banished Frenchman lashed by broken fortunes and hope's failures, springs to his feet at its mention, makes of his last coin a thank-offering in its honor, and repeats it proudly in the very chancel of God's temple, amid the homage of worshipers. It is the synonym of the people's governor, the people's choice against hereditary monarchy. The fires of liberty are in it, and the France that he reclaimed will never down at a king's bidding for any long period. Her licentiousness and infidelity are dying, and as she drinks in the pure life of Christian faith and principle she will rise to Christian liberty and equality. Her sentiment is the American sentiment, and their eagles have been in sympathy since hers brought to ours, in its conflict with kingly tyranny, her diplomacy and treasure and blood. Were Napoleon living now, he would be the *president*, not the emperor, of the French. The name Napoleon will survive that of Bourbon. The name Napoleon will survive that of emperor."

CHAPTER XXVIII.

WITH SONGFUL WINDS AMONGST THE BOWING FLOWERS.

 KNOW not which was merriest in camp that night because of Tom's letter's estimate of me. Mack, especially after his Napoleonic rocket, seemed to vie with Wyche and Maine in helping me to remember it. And you may have been waiting for some token of my "feeling" about it. Feeling. Well, feeling. But you know Tom. Yet I think he believed about as he wrote. But when the stars blinked midnight to us from their swinging beds we were all awake. For Maine, who had snored a solo an hour and more, seemed as fresh as we who had idled most of the day.

The smoke from an Indian camp floated over a ridge and settled in the ravines north of us; the rivulet leaped over the little falls, but was too dry to make much fuss about it; and the donkey waking the echoes, crawled nearer the fire and, lying down, watched us pretty much as a fine old mastiff would have done; while I, in memory of Tom and the brown donkey, took him a loaf of bread, and staid by him till he ate it. I returned to the group as Wyche said:

"Tom, however, is not alone in egotism, by many. They are met on campus, platform, bench, in the temple of justice, in that of mercy, on the deck at sea; almost everywhere they appear whose god is egotism. You refuse to resent the absurdities of the god because of the virtues amid which unhappily he is throned. With such a one whatever good is wrought or evil avoided, *he* did it, however trifling the part he enacted. Nothing is that he could not have bettered, and to all that is his connection therewith imparts all of worth that attaches. He looks up at the capitol's dome; it is an architectural marvel, but not before he beheld it. The look he cast to it invested it with the pencilings of genius, and, he rather thinks, built and paid for it. He is drowned in the surf; you bear him to the strand, recall him to life; he saved himself—just then had conquered the wave when you uselessly grasped him. You find him unknown, herald him to fame, make for him opportunity, cluster honors upon him; *he* did it himself. He is as oblivious of your handiwork in his fortunes as the world is of that of editors in supplying, directing, and wreathing its brain with honors.

"If he speaks, the eloquence of Demosthenes is eclipsed, that of Webster a baseless vision. If he battles, though it be with a wisp of cobwebs, the day was the bloodiest, the slain countless. His definition of something is himself; of nothing, the world without him. You do not disturb his conceit by bursting his bubble; yet you feel that egotism, though set in a coronet, tarnishes the brilliance and repels like a serpent coiled among flowers. Retaining your attachment for the man, you excuse him by laughing at the god. 'That god, Egotism!' you say, and forgive his assumacy."

"You could better tolerate him," said Maine, "if he were satisfied with self-puffing. But he as certainly detracts from others as he exaggerates himself. He outlines his own picture on a large scale, and much overcolors it; and draws others' pictures in a cramped scale, and much overshades them."

"Taking others' pictures is a delightful art," said Mack, " if numbers devoted to it are good evidence. Nearly all are artists in this line, each esteeming himself 'an old master.' If the pictures they paint with lip and pen are 'true to life,' this world hath in it saints but one,

16

devils all beside; nobody's great, good, but one, and he guides the pencil. Ah! here the rub is. Egotism, or a god like him, inspires the artist to shade deeply every picture save his own, and this the vision of his own fancy. But as he too is painted by another, we will find him grouped somewhere, a scowling reprobate like all the rest. Only if man had made man, what a wonderful piece of mechanism he would have been! But as God made him, and in his own likeness, he's but a meager beast at best. True enough, he is much marred by the devil, and himself far bent from the original design; but surely he has not been defaced of all the touch divine. They must see him through a glass, darkly, or their pictures would have more light, less shadow, except when extremes are brought upon the easel."

The points of fire that, at intervals, had been coming this side the ridge from the Indian camp, like magnified points of stars thrust through the fissured ravines nearest its top, had widened and lengthened and run round, and met in the narrower spaces here and there, till it appeared like many islands floating in estuaries of flame. And the wind, setting in from us thither, pushed the encircling flames rapidly upward till the tops of the ridge appeared

like illuminated cones of rock and plant sink-
ing in the roaring billows of the burning sea.
We beheld the unusual spectacle with bated
breath. And as from her lair a brown bear
with her cubs started this way and that, and
climbed to the summit, and watched the encircling flames on all sides, our hearts hushed
beating in the concern we felt for the poor
beasts. But a few moments decided the anx-
ious mother; and placing her paw caressingly
upon each of her twins for an instant, she
turned down to a point where the fiery estuary
was narrowest, and, lying down, rolled over it,
followed by the imitative cubs. An involuntary shout rang from our throats as we recognized the grandness of motherhood displayed
in the bear. And as just below the circle of
heat she paused on a broad, fire-lit rock in
safety, and licked and fondled and played with
the cubs, the soft, sweet scenes of mother's
love and delighted tenderness in trouble and
in joy touched our hearts; and as, presently, she
pierced the unburning chapparal nearing the
little stream a hundred yards below us, the
cubs about her, huzza after huzza greeted her;
and she turned down into the cool gulch, and
was safe again. When the conversation that
the scene and incident had interrupted was re-

sumed, the voices were softer, as though out
of the wildness of flame and beast had come a
sprite of gentleness, imparting to us a reverence for every thing that God had made. And
Wyche said:

"There is but one 'Master' whose pictures
are without a mistake—God. All lights and
shades he paints us in are faultless; and we do
well to receive them without question. In him
is a skill that, discerning our rippling penitence and faith, transfers us to the canvas so
robed in these that our pictures glow with joy
for heaviness, light for shadow, the hue of life
for that of death, and yet is true to life.

"But of no other is that he paints of you
true because *he* paints it. His, at best, is de-
fective skill, blemishing its pictures with its
own imperfections."

"Man is unfitted to paint man," said Maine.
"He will denounce if life be assassinated, yet
thrust the treacherous blade into its reputation. He is emulous of good, but not when
good is evil spoken of. He is ambitious of
success, but accounts this applause; and to
gain it will appropriate another's deserving or
minify it, and magnify his fault. He will approve a character, yet assails it if so wags the
world. If Christ bear the cross, not the crown,

he'll jeer him without the city, and jeer him for a devil, though he is God. He discerns virtue, yet is so selfish he will detract from it to attract to himself, or dash the gem to pieces, lest, himself unadorned by it, it should adorn another. His friendship is graceful when to bestow it is profitable to him, but to *stay* one struggling with adversities and contempts is too strange a fire for him to warm at."

"Yet," said Wyche, "with all his devilism there is something God-like in man; but it requires God to bring it out. An angel would become impatient with him; a fiend would fall away from the task in ecstasy, and say, 'He's good enough for me; very like my brother;' man would caricature him by distortion and embellishment; only God sees him as he is, and is adequate to accurately picture one so lapsed, yet so advanced. Dipping his pencil in the blood of Christ, he blushes sick humanity with so sweet virtues that it shines on the verge of hell like a scintillation of heaven, enlights for the skies, and spheres there. The lip is hesitant to drop the blood of Jesus often lest the pearl of fathomless merit 'fall among swine.' But who that notes the soft lines, nice lights, and pure shades with which that purple Pearl touches man but has his numbed being startled into reverential amaze, aspires to be vivified by it, and utilized to purity and good?"

Maine here said something about the pulpit's neglect of Jesus, its familiarity with philosophies and oppositions of science, its unfamiliarity with Biblicism; and expressed himself so pertinently, yet so considerately, that we were about to lose our picture topic. But Mack woke up as out of a dream, and said:

"The art of taking others' likenesses has tripped down to us, petted by clanging ages, from gray antiquity. More than thirty centuries ago an old Arabic papyrus was unrolled before the eager eyes of sages, whose words, like floods of honey, and anon like floods of aloe, leaped down the channel of time, are leaping still, telling of a picture painted by three renowned artists of this school. Many would be familiar with this scroll but for a malady that has preyed upon the priestly line that, as Maine says, 'hath cankered the surplice and nearly eaten out of it the image and superscription of Jesus, and the word whose entrance giveth light.' It says:

"There was a man in the land of Uz whose substance was very great. The young men and the aged, the princes and the nobles, reverenced him. When the ear heard him then it blessed him, and the eye when it saw him gave witness to him; because he delivered the poor that cried, and the fatherless, and him that had none to help him; and caused the widow's heart to sing for joy. He was eyes to the blind, and feet was he to the lame; and a father to the poor, though he had a great family of his own to provide for.

"He waited not for suffering to report itself ere he relieved it, but the cause he knew not he searched out. He brake the jaws of the wicked, and plucked the spoil out of his teeth. He neither feared a great multitude, nor did the contempt of families terrify him. Nor rejoiced he at the destruction of him that hated him, nor walked with vanity, nor hasted to deceit. Unto him men gave ear, kept silent at his counsel, waited for his words as for the rain; for righteousness clothed him, and his judgment was a robe and a diadem. He sat chief, and dwelt as a king in the army, as *one that comforteth the mourners.*

"But adversity came to him. His children in a day suddenly died, and all his fortunes vanished. An evil disease gat hold upon him, and he lay desolate in ashes. Then fell away from him his friends, except his wife, and she, in sympathy's delirium, bade him curse God and die. They that were younger than he, whose fathers he would have disdained to have sit with the dogs of his flock, had him in derision. They who were driven forth from among men, and cut up mallows and juniper roots for their meat, and brayed in the bushes, children of fools, viler than the earth, made him their song and their by-word, and spared not to spit upon him.

"On the right rose the youth; they pushed away his feet, they marred his path, they set forward his calamities. Terrors turned upon him and pursued his soul. His bones were pierced in the night season, and his sinews took no rest. His bowels boiled and rested not, and his skin grew black upon him, while his bones burned with heat; for Satan kindled fires within him, and without burned him with reproach, until he became brother to dragons. And his heart also was turned to mourning, and his organ into the voice of them that weep.

"Then came the three princes, his friends, to take his picture, and, uniting their skill, produced a portraiture of him so perfect, they thought, they hung it in the Hall Inspiration. Its expression was irreverent folly, cruel op-

pression, treachery, selfishness, hypocrisy. And
this was the title they wrote upon it: 'Job,
great in wickedness, in iniquity infinite.'

"Then the Almighty appeared. The solemn mountains laughed, the little hills skipped
for joy, and the glad sunshine knelt down
with the songful winds amongst the bowing
flowers, delightedly chanting Alleluia with
happy earth and the shouting sky. So he too
looked for good, but evil came; waited for
light, but came darkness; and he coiled down
lower in dust and ashes, and said: 'Behold, I
am vile!' and scraping himself with a potsherd,
wept. His three painters passed by and said:
'Aha! aha!' But God came even unto him, and
stooped down and touched him, and said: 'My
servant, Job, there is none like him in the
earth; a perfect and an upright man, one that
feareth God and escheweth evil, *and still he
holdeth fast his integrity.* Pray for *them,* for my
wrath is kindled against them to deal with
them after their folly.' And in his black woe
he prayed for his friends, and the Lord turned
the captivity of Job while he prayed; also the
Lord gave Job twice as much as he had before.

"In the meanwhile Truth, while passing
through the art-gallery of Hall Inspiration,
beheld his picture placed there by his three

friends, and, blushing at the caricature, went
to heaven's portfolio, and brought thence the
portrait she had painted of him, and hung it
above the other without note or comment.
Repairing to the hall one day with beautiful
Charity to return it to the portfolio as heav-
en's favorite, she found it nailed by the Master of assemblies immovably to the wall, and
this inscription in the handwriting of God: 'A
perfect and an upright man.' And they bowed
their graceful forms, and worshiped God who
judgeth righteous judgment.

"'Truth,' said Charity, 'we do err who
judge by appearances. The prince of Uz insisted that his friends were picturing him inaccu-
rately, and I whispered as much oft in their
ears. But the *evil* they thought they painted,
and called it after the perfect man.'

"'Charity,' replied Truth, 'to err is common with man. If there is any better in erring
it is found in lighting, not shading, a picture.
Let us, as we go from this pure hall, in its
loving inspiration persuade men not to sur-
mise evil of their neighbor, nor to think more
highly of themselves than they ought to,
and so avoid taking inaccurate portraits.
Failing this, let us persuade the neighbor not
to be distressed by their caricatures, but to

stand in his lot, his proper character, regardless of their fond conceits, till the end be.

"And they passed forth on their mission."

CHAPTER XXIX.

THIS KING OF THE WEST—ON THE SHAPE CAME CLINGING.

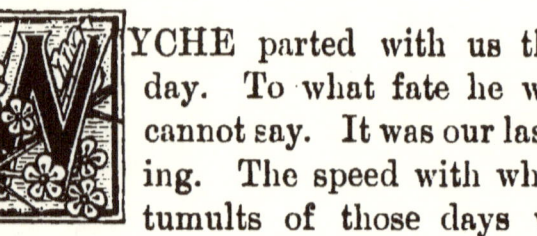YCHE parted with us the next day. To what fate he went we cannot say. It was our last meeting. The speed with which the tumults of those days whirled persons apart, and forever hid them from each other, was like that with which Norway's mythic sea-whirl swallows the boatman and his boat to be seen no more. And to what numbers and wonders the gold-field maelstrom sucked under its unfortunates is a story that perhaps others will partly unfold, and there will be wizzardry in it. From friend hidden to stranger revealed was an oft-told tale in the golden phantasms that hurled us together and tossed us apart in the ruder days of the California gold-hunt.

Maine was energetic, saving, yet generous and good-humored. He loathed nothing but an Indian, and despised nothing but a negro, for whose freedom he was ready to *argue* whenever he could do so without loss of time from gold-gathering. He would not endure a darky's cookery—always sweeter to Mack and me than any other—and contact with him his honest abolition heart abhorred. When we specially hungered for something good to eat, and called in black Sam, who said he was "from Massysip," and pretended to mine, with others, half a mile below us, and gave him the freedom of our larder to get up the best feast he could, Maine would spend the day down in the claim.

When dinner was ready on such occasions, old Sam's "Halloo!" would rollick through the mine, and though Maine would neither heed it nor our "Come, let's to that feast," he never demurred to the programme. "Every one to his taste," he would say, and work away contentedly. At first when we came without Maine and sat down to the washed log and scoured tins, and savory dishes of old Sam's skill, he would say, "Whar's Mas Maine?"

Mack answered, "This is his fast-day."

The old shine grunted a disapproval, but said nothing. The next time, the same question and answer drew from him the comment: "He cust turrer day, an' cussin' an' fastin' doan 'long togedder." It was duly reported to Maine, with such flourishes as Mack thought fit to improvise.

About the fifth occasion of the sort he asked no questions for several minutes, but sat near upon a stump watching with great satisfaction as morsel after morsel played hide-and-seek between our lips. As he filled our tins with the third pour of his delicious coffee, he said: "Wha' dat Mister Chunk; he doan come eat he dinner?"

"Who?" queried we.

"Dat chunk you partner wid," he answered.

"O," replied Mack, "he's gouging a speck of gold out of a piece of cement, and is afraid it will jump out and hide if all leave the mine. But, Sam, he's more like the ridge-pole of a cabin than like a chunk."

"No, sah," he answered; "he like nutting dat 'longs to a cabin. He like de 'ceevin' chunk 'cross de by-yore; you step on 'im, thinks yer gwine 'cross safe; he role over, drap you in de water fur drown. He think nigger skin too blarck fur 'im to eat arter. Nigger heart whiter'n his'n, an' he skin ain't much blarcker."

Here Maine came round the tent corner. Old Sam never budged, but a queer grin wrinkled his face as he said: "You bofe better eat dem brown pieces; he done mighty parfect."

I said, "Fix Chunk's place."

And Maine, whose face glinted with pleasantry, having overheard Sam's comments, christened his new name, Chunk, by which he went thereafter in the diggings, by a meal that would have done credit to Tom in the early stage of his nostalgic attack. Sam seemed never so happy as when attending to our feasts, and always said, "I charges nuffin." But Chunk said the reason was he knew that was the way to double wages. He often came unbidden to the camp, never unwelcomed, and went away with a glad step, for he went full-handed, and I may add full-hearted. For at least Mack appeared to know precisely how to cheer and fill him with sunshine, and yet seemed never to try to do so. And Chunk, too, learned how to make him glad, but often said, "I wouldn't live in a land of niggers for the hull South."

Already the hoar-frost was shivering upon every green thing and every damp spot. The heights woke up of mornings with veils of vapor tucked around their heads; the slopes smoked with heavy mists; and along the rivulet's chasmy course, and up each gorge, clouds of fog tottered slowly, to melt away in the clear ether nearer heaven. So we knew gruff winter would soon build citadels of ice, and spread thick wastes of snow about us. But the phantom of gold sung to us out of the mists and wintry signals as musically as though April's buds were popping about us, and spelled us to the spot.

Fifty feet above the streamlet the stubborn granite jutted widely out from the mountain-side; and Maine and I having agreed to spend the winter there, Mack, before leaving, helped us drift a large room under the granite. We closed the front with heavy pickets, hedged it with deeply planted cedars, and corded firewood, and stored it with provisions.

Mack bid us good-by. But he said, as he stood in the trail ready to start: "I will write from San Francisco, then from New Orleans. I hope you shall be as happy and successful as my heart wishes, and as my life with you both has been pleasant." And he turned down the trail, and was hidden by the jungle.

Maine said, as his eyes followed him out of sight: "Before the associations of this copartnership, I felt that the Northern and the Southern man were the contrary the one of the other, each the other's reverse, no harmony, nor could be. But these are only prejudices—hidden rocks fretting the waters of the heart that should be blown out, or sunk through to China. Why will the heart be a jagged-bottomed archipelago where counter-currents dash, instead of the quiet deep where we float with a sense of security and peace? Mack's a world of good feeling and pure principle; quick, but too courteous to be on the offensive."

November floundered carelessly upon the mountains. Its glad suns, its cool moons, its quiet and holiday airs, its changing leaves and falling, its occasional mists, its Indian-summery warmths interrupted now and then by the winds upon rampages, and soughing or whistling afterward, as the humor was, filled us with a diversity of emotions as delightful as were the physical sensations they imparted. And in the mine a richer vein had been cut, and we were pursuing its golden run and catching its golden drops in shovel and pan and girdle, and storing them in a secreting-vault convenient of defense, if not defiant of discovery. And so we toiled in the glow of hope realized, and often in the zest forgot breakfast; and dug and washed and laid by in the sun to gleam and dry, the little and larger

17

nuggets, till high noon laughed at us from the dun skies; a hurried dinner, and then till twilight nodded into night, when we supped and slept to awake with the light and repeat the days that had just passed. But any old miner could have told us "it could not last;" either we would give out, or the vein. In this instance it was both. But in the three weeks our vault had received nearly five hundred ounces on deposit, and we were now tranquilly hunting the vein again.

As Maine scaled the steep with a bucket of water one noon to the narrow belt of plateau that clung about our granite room, a herd of deer leaped from near our hedge, and fleeing along the mountain-side a few hundred yards, browsed as if oblivious of us. He reported that an Indian tribe was gathering at the mine, and would break things to pieces, he feared. But a glance revealed that there were but twenty or thirty of the forest kings, and these not bent on mischief. One of them lounged up to the tent, and said: "Whizkee, tam, coot."

Maine replied by showing him an empty bottle. He smelled it and said with emphasis: "No smell; whizkee not, tam. No want 'em."

And as he turned away, Maine said: "And

so this king of the West has taken on two touches of Anglo-American civilization—profanity and love of whisky. How rapid the spread of vice! how easily, as to it born, the heart gives it bed and board!"

California appeared to grow bottles in those days. They were met with everywhere. The towns, highways, trails, plains, valleys, hidden fastnesses, peaks, trees, were sprinkled with bottles. If Humboldt had delayed his "Cosmos" till then, he likely would have written:

"The peculiarity of this section of the earth is its chief fruit, b. bottles, which crop out upon its diversified surface in vast quantities and many varieties; odor, whisky. Occupations, filling and emptying bottles. The inhabitants are industrious; day and night they may be seen lying, sitting, squatting, standing, in houses, on roads and trails, on pathless plains and mountains, on peak-tops, in abysses, holding the big ends of bottles toward the sky, small ends growing to their lips, their throats gurgling, swallows in lively commotion. I saw some of the population otherwise employed. Instance, Maine and his partner. But they had bottles, *empty.* Inference, bottles here grow to human lips; fall when empty; *many* fall, almost instantly; replaced by larger ones, if possible. At Bottletown, back in the Sierras, is a great pine whose cap bud is a bottle—bottom up, of course. Query: Do the very trees here drink whisky? Name of section suggested: Bottellas Infinitas."

We directed the Indians to the deer. And immediately each red man, with bow and arrow, glided up a ravine to be in position when the herd should dash down it; for one had been sent to turn them thither. Two of the startled creatures were mortally wounded by the clumsy arrows of the red bowmen, and fell on the opposite mountain, whence, amid many genuflections, the overjoyed Indians hurried with the carcases into wilder gloom among the loftier heights northward. And as they dipped behind a spur beyond view, Maine exclaimed, "What is uncultured man but a wonderful or a ridiculous beast?"

The snow had come again, and its leaps and falls and somersaults and gyratory recoils and tumbles over the whitened world about us made us to rejoice that our drift for gold had led us into a tunnel, where we could toil unhindered by its thickening tempest for awhile. But soon it beat us out of that by closing its mouth and snowing it under, and freezing down upon it and every thing, in thick, vast, wavy folds, as though the world had emptied a century of its cotton crop about us, and the fleecy thing were stunned with wonder at the "tumble" it had had at last, and were dying here amid groaning forests, and the soft notes of its child-flakes coming to rest upon its bosom in the mighty stretch of frozen jungle.

To-night the sky had cleared. Moon and stars, and the spaces of blue between them, seemed to be throwing down upon white-robed earth irrepressible congratulations for the simple purity of her dress, and in their rayed joys and earth's white light objects in the thin air appeared strange and bewitching to the eye. Maine had gone from the tent for an armful of kindling he had prepared for morning, or midnight uses on demand, and called me out to notice a man on the mountain-side opposite the camp. He was in three hundred feet of us, though he would have to come as many yards to reach us. The gait, air, shape, size, stride, motion were Pike's, and I said, "Pike's ghost."

Maine glanced at me keenly. I think Tom's letter came back to him then, and he thought it was true as it said "Crazy;" but it said also, "He can't help his brains;" nor I couldn't.

But on the shape came, clinging there to an iced sappling, and there to a jutting iced rock, and there sliding, and then slipping about but not falling; and now it stood and threw an eager look across the chasm to us, and said, "Is Quien over thar?"

I had a thought of denying my name—the voice was Pike's; but I answered readily enough for so cold a night: "Yes. Cross just above where you stand, if you *do* stand."

But, with his old-time daring, he skated down to the rivulet's bed just where he was, where I met him to show him, politely as possible, the best way up to our room in the rock. He looked at me closely with the old-time look a moment in the moonshine when we got together on the stream's frozen, shivering face, and said: "It's you, sartin; nothin' onbeauti-fuller in natur' 'cept Tom."

It was Pike, soul and body; and I began to think, "May be it's the resurrection coming on;" but he grasped me by the arm like a vise, yet his hand trembled too, and his eyes were misty withal, as he said: "I've come a long way ter shake your hand, for poor Racket's sake. Tom gin me your pictur' more'n a year ago, when he were gittin onto the steamer fur the States. It's *you*, I know."

" Yes," said I, " I believe it is, is, *now*. Come up to the camp." And he nearly carried me up the steep.

He toasted himself before the fire, precisely as I had seen Pike do many times; every feature, the entire physique, manner, tone, language, glance, smile, was Pike from under the cairn. "It's Pike," I thought again. But I asked him if he and Racket were kin.

" Kin?" he said; " yes; *Racket and me's the same.*" Here the pause was a period, and Maine glanced at me questioningly; but he added in a soft melody of voice: " Leastwise Racket and me is twin-brothers. He writ me much of you and Tom afore you laid him away under the rocks to rest till judgment. God bless you for it, stranger! I've been to his grave, and the manzanita hev locked hands over it, like the very bushes loved him.

" I've got a ranch in Sacramento Valley; an' you must go spend the winter with me. I come arter you a purpose. You'll friz inter ice here, an' now Tom's gone, you are bound ter be the onlikeliest lump thar is. This is my third trip a-huntin' on you. A fellow named Wyche wer tellin' a red-whiskered doctor in Sacramento four days ago 'bout your'n an' Tom's crazy scrape; an' I ax'd him ef he knowed whar a friend could find yer right away. An' he said, 'In twenty mile o' Downieville, more or less.' Thar a packer told me you were in these diggin's some'rs, fur he 'd brought you a kergo o' grub a month ago."

"You have suffered in the icy tramp," I said, "but we have a supper ready for you; the steaming coffee will impart *some* warmth. But how did you and Tom become known to each other?"

There was a smile, the humorous smile of Pike, on his face at the question, but his voice was tender as a girl's while repeating the first sentence or two, as he answered: "Mother were allus a-lookin' out the door in ole Missouri fur Racket ter come down the road from Californy; but he never come. She did n't live long arter we got Racket's package yer sent when he died; and the letter you writ were in her bosom when she were dyin'; an' we buried it with her. So I moved west, an' kept a-movin' till I got to San Francisco. I'd been thar a few days, at the Tremont, when a fat, red-faced chap kept a pryin' into my face. Wharever I were thar he were a-lookin' at me like crazy. So I went inter the streets, but thar he were a follerin' an' a-starein' at me. I went ter the wharf among the ships, an' at every turn he'd be a-watchin' on me. I got tired on it, an' went up to him, at last, an' said: 'Look a-here, you'ev been arter me long enough. Do you want any thing o' me?'

" 'Yes,' he said, 'yes I do. I want to know whar you come from, who you are, and all about you.'

" ' Waal,' said I, 'I come from old Missouri, kin take care of myself, an' my name's Jim · Knight.' His eye sparkled soft-like, and he laid his hand on my shoulder, and said: 'It's Racket's brother, ef it *ain't* himself.' And then I had to stay in his room, an' go whar he went, an' be right with him until he got on the steamer fur Panama. That unor'nary chap *loved* Racket teetotally."

Jim tarried with us several days, enlivened the hours with anecdote and song, hunted in the "frizen things;" and his rifle-shots were fatal to several deer and bears, which he salted down for us in a "smokeus," he called it, that he dug out for us in the back of our room. When he left us he said: "You won't ranch it with me nohow. But mind, ef ever misfortin gits the uppermost on you, manage to let me know, an' I'll be with yer like lightnin'. You were clever to Racket, an' I wish I could bring yer 'tarnal joy fur it."

"Fraternal love," said Maine, "lodged in a man's heart is a fresh and noble grace. It has survived bitter experiences. It comes to cheer when the burdens oppress, when sorrows have pierced, when passions have scorched, when wrongs have filled with thorns of poison and pain. To me Joseph is in no instance greater than when, rendering excuse for the sin of his brothers against him, he takes them out of their poverty and famine, and enriches and ennobles them. The selfish Egyptian courtier, possibly, sneered at the deed and feeling; but the angels said, 'It is love—it makes him like God,' and, catching fire from next the throne, sped from heaven and anointed him with immortality. Such a one rises to Jim Knight's sentiment: 'You were clever to my brother, and if ever misfortune gets the uppermost of you, manage to let me know, and I will be with you like lightning.'"

I liked Maine the better for his fresh, bright words; and felt I was a boy again paddling about in fraternal love. It is winsome in a boy's heart. It links him to his little brother's griefs and joys, so he helps him carry his burdens, lifts him over the fence too high for him, across the stream too broad for him, shelters him from the tyranny of big boys, shares with him his fruits, fish-hooks, and marbles; lets him roll his hoop, spin his top, bounce his ball, prance his hoop-horse, play his Jew's-harp, june his June-bug; and when he falls and hurts himself, helps him up, saying: "Never mind little brother, you'll be well to-morrow, and we'll have a jolly time *together.*"

CHAPTER XXX.

BOLLS OF BERYL AND GOLD.

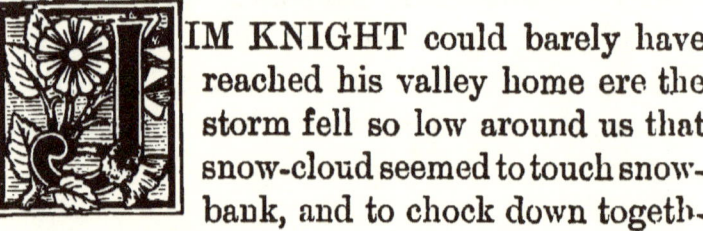

IM KNIGHT could barely have reached his valley home ere the storm fell so low around us that snow-cloud seemed to touch snow-bank, and to chock down together into the gorge, and to mourn the fall of a frantic uproar of whirring, whizzing wails. Much of the snow melted as it fell, or was mingled with rain, so each ravine flowed down torrents to the chasm at our feet, and the rivulet fretted and foamed along its icy channel till it became an angry river, uprooting trees, knocking the clay props from under granite masses, and rolling them along its ragged course, till the grinding of the rocks, the splash and rumble of the floods, and the majestic call of storm to storm were a grand chant that made the awful jungle appear like a temple of ice being set apart to the service of Him who "giveth snow like wool, scattereth the hoar-frost like ashes, casteth forth his ice like morsels, sendeth out his word and melteth them, causeth the wind to blow, and the waters to flow." By sundown the river had lifted its turbulent floods within a dozen feet of the plateau, and uprooted trees, whirling on the stream, threw out their arms and tore the tough cedars from the brink and swung out with them to voyage the surging waters. Fragments of flumes shooting by on the flashing current told us of troubled miners on tributary gulches, of hope bereaved, lost in the gathering of the waters. But as the cold increased we knew that every flake was freezing with each streamlet, and the river that thundered against our bluff had done its worst.

The changes in the tempest were signaled to us by its voices. When it was sleeping, and only the air filled the spaces between earth and cloud, only the voices of the blood seemed to be pouring in the ear their softest melodies as though with them were the quietest strains of song that ever soothes its flow, and the purest that ever chastens its flames; and a quieting was on the senses, and in the heart too, how we couldn't discern, but we were strangely, quietly content.

When it was only snowing through the spaces, it seemed that tiny whispers, like sweetest sighs perishing, just appreciable to the ear, were about us, and a rustling in the air, soft as the falling of downiest feathers, that made the ear dream that it heard the faintest possible echoes of far-off multitudes of tiniest wings, removing farther and farther, coming, coming nearer and nearer, now gone, now returned, coming, going, intermixing incessantly, never near enough to be distinctly heard, never far enough away to be out of hearing longer than a few moments.   Or when it was pouring snow-flakes, the sound was like one imagines the voice of silence is when flowing softest through the ice-bells hanging on millions of fragile twigs, making music so indefinable that one might think it the notes of the stars singing, straying too far away, together fading into nothing.

When it displaced the snow with sleet, there was a clear, whizzy ringing in the air distinctly heard, yet the tiniest and most musical ringing notes the ear can discern, and a merry little shattering above and all about that makes the nerves freshen with the thought that the ringing sleet is a company of headlong fledgeling boys coming to a merry-making with the snow-flakes, that are girls.   And, too, now and then there is a gliding and a rattling that make us think the merry imps are leaping down off the twigs, or climbing out upon them to shake the icicles off to hear them crash, and see them skate down the hills.

When the tempest filled the spaces with rain we knew it by the splash. When it broke into storms, the winds fly and growl and howl and whistle and dance and rush, and the clouds are seemingly breaking into one another's munitions of rain and ice, carrying each other by storm; the forest mourns, the rocks scream, the gorges roar, the mountains bellow, a tremor shakes the ground, limbs crack and fly from their places, and forest-kings fall along the earth with lumbering sounds like signal-guns of distress at sea, and all is commotion without and awe within.

All night long beast signaled beast in the elemental mélée; and once a brave push was made against our picket door, answered by a flight of bullets through the cracks, and the animal leaped wildly away and plunged, we knew by the splashing thud, out into the tumultuous river, and we heard it buffeting the contrary currents, then fiercely roar far down on the other side.

The next morning a band of Indians straggled near us, picking their way southward. We beckoned them to the camp and gave them

much of the venison that Jim had salted down
for us; and as one gathered a firebrand and
moved on, they defiled after him, stolidly bearing the pieces of flesh to a sheltered dell.
Soon, by the columns of smoke and bursts of
whoop and laughter, we knew they were in
high carnival, though the snowy storm beat
upon them.

They had barely feasted and skirred across
the spur next them when a few old men and
women and little children came on tottering
step, following in their trail. Maine feasted
them upon remnants of bread and venison that
had been accumulating for several days, made
them a bucket of coffee, loaded them with
fresh meat, and they tottered out into the tempest again. He stood a long while watching
their old bare heads, grizzled by age and white
with snow, with the tripping children bare of
clothing, tramping by their side. When he
turned into the tent, I said: "If those old
foresters were Southern slaves, such weather
as this they would be warmly clad, in good
cabins, round a big fire broiling bacon,
cooking ash-cakes and potatoes and that
best of dishes, lye-hominy, laughing, singing, happy; and the lads and lasses, gone
on before, would be doing likewise, spicing

the programme by snugly courting. Which had you rather be, a Southern darky or one of them?"

"I ca'c'late," he replied, "the darky is the most comfortable; but I'd rather be one of them, *free* to defy the storm when too thriftless to own a shelter to warm in out of it."

In the meanwhile the Indian is passing on, as he has been for centuries—passing from sea to sea, through all climes, through forests and mountains and delightful valleys, the child of the jungle, in savagery still, fleeing civilization, unblessed by its virtues, cursed by its vices—passing on till there is no region beyond into which he may pass.

We have founded temples and schools upon the mounds of his storied dead, tamed his lakes and rivers and wilds with steam, and hustled him out of his valleys and fastnesses with our industries. We need and will have his whole domain for good uses, are bound to light up its recesses with electricity so not a recess can he hide in; and our roving families kill the grizzly because he kills their stock and their children, and will kill him for the same reason. What shall we do with him? Discrown him for his own good, and for ours as well; make a citizen of him, give him the bal-

18

lot, make him subject to the laws to which we are subjected; and he will be still long enough to be civilized.

About three o'clock one afternoon we were startled, while standing on the bluff in front of the camp, by a volley of icicles rattling down the mountain and shivering to pieces around us. We watched up the height to detect the animal that had loosened them, but all was quiet for a minute or two. Then other icicles came rushing down from a projecting snow-bank a thousand yards from us, and nearly twice as many feet above us, and Maine saying, "Sleet melting this sunny weather," we turned to discuss our claim again. But a minute later, an awful, grating, roaring, hissing, flitting sound quickly drew our eyes cragward to see a mountain of snow, limbs, and rocks, like a monster wave of white lightning and furious thunders, bounding down upon us. We fled like arrows beneath our rock to avoid the avalanche. It swept athwart our rock-roofed room, and buried itself in the chasm below with a horrible roar, having torn away most of our little plateau. Its white race-track was about three hundred feet wide. As it rushed over our rock-roof its sound was unutterably grating, *quick*, fierce, stunning, like the irking roar of a thousand steamers vying in letting off steam together.

We were prone upon the clay floor, faces in our palms, when it passed over us, some impulse we noted not having cast us down so, when we entered beneath the rocks. When he sat up, the first words Maine uttered were: "Sakes alive! Whew!" To which I replied: "Sh—, sh—, shucks!"

Now and then till sundown snow-scales were shaken from the locks of the crags tumbling toward the chasm, and, however small when first discovered coming down the mountain, wound about themselves icicles and soft snow till they were large as cabins. Many of them butted their brains out against the trees in the descent, breaking on to the gorge in many fragment, like mad children of the avalanche bounding to their mother on her chasmy bed. The winds rose after night-fall and beat against the mountains, and packed with its millions of blows the snow-banks hard again, and chilled them there with freezing blasts.

When the spring thaw came, it was charming to dwell in this city of snow. Bursting from under its gleamy minarets and streets of ice, many water-spouts jetted crystal rills into the rivulet, till tower after tower melted down,

palaces fell in, cottages crumbled and, with the
icy pavements, flowed away, bearing to the
dwellers in the valleys the refreshing snow-
floods.   The sides of the mountains more and
more looked like patch-work—here a space of
white, there of dark, yonder of green, and intermingled stretches of flowers.   For flowers
and green grasses often kissed the snow-circles,
and green leaves fluttered above it, till in the
July days the earth-border reached from the
placer of toil to old Winter's palace on the
peak.   And soon the sunbeams up there print-
ing leaves and twiggy shadows on its weeping face, it melted away in their warm caresses, and, like Aaron's golden calf, turned to
dust; it was "strewed upon the water," and
the tribes " drink of it."

In August our rich lead was lost beyond
tracing.   We had, however, made a " pile " of
many ounces of virgin gold; and Maine departed for the Atlantic States; and as the
" tiredness," of which my first gold-field partner so often lectured, clung to me still, I concluded to visit among the valleys to breathe
awhile their softer airs, and enjoy their milk
and honey and fruits and restfulness.

I left the stage at the Mokelumne River to
strike across the plains to the Calaveras Valley,

about sixteen miles distant. The stroll was a
joy to me. The dust of the beaten road, the
clatter of coach and team and passengers were
an annoyance. They were gone; and walking
across the brown plains among scattered herds
and flocks, and humming bees, and leaping rabbits, brought me nearer home than I had been
for many months, even in scenic associations.
Night came on before I could get to the ranch
where an old friend dwelt. The stars shone
merrily, however, and the moon flooded my
pathless route as I neared the blue belt of
timber that marked the course of the little
winding river that named the valley. Bancroft Library

In crossing a low roll of knolls, I beheld in
the distance many lights like spectral stars
grouped near the ground, arched by a leafy
sea of green at rest in some wide-boughed
trees. They laughed in my face, whirled
round, moved to and fro, intermingled as if
whispering together, stood still stretching
their eyes at me as if wondering why I stopped
on the brown turf watching them before passing down the knoll; and the foliaged dome and
its branchy, angulated rafters tossed about in
a silvery illumination as breezes shook them
above the solitary aisles of the strange temple. It was nothing to me, whatever it was, I

thought, and journeyed on among the dips and rises of the plain. But presently in a little vale, still shut in from the lights, I was arrested by song as of many voices, and was spelled to the spot. It chimed in the air, paused at my feet, rippled through my hair, touched my pack till it was light as a feather, echoed on my cheeks, whispered in my ears, lodged on my breast, got into my heart, and out in tears at my eyes; and scaling the knoll I saw that the temple of leaves had become a temple of God where a thousand worshipers were praising him, at a California camp-meeting. Involuntarily thither I went.

The clear heavens, that autumnal night, were dressed in silvery tissue over azure skirts clustered with stars; and dark-eyed earth lay marveling at their beauty. Zephyr's step was muffled, and every few minutes she sighed up to the skies, and, invisible, flitted here and there among the worshipers, and whispered to the green leaves above them. And the silent company's eyes looked like spirits hearkening for heavenly signs, as they intently fastened upon the minister. He spoke of the ruin sin brings to persons and peoples, its stains indelible to all except Christ's blood; how lovingly he would save us, and surely, only if we would

come to him. Come all; come now; trust, obey.
The worst need not hesitate; he died for the
chief of sinners, died that we might not perish, but might have life. The "pearl of great
price"—everybody's, yours; brighter than gold-
en ore—saving love! it will make you happy
here, hereafter.

The hush upon the congregation had been
awesome, and many seemed to be in the thrall
of a wand, at whose touch the gold-phantom's
charm dissolved, and left them dreaming of
the "gold tried in the fire," resolved in all
their seeking to seek *that.* As the service
closed, a person whom I had not noticed, leaning against the same tree with me, murmured:
"Simple, clear, sensible, persuasive. If Leina
had been here she would have enjoyed it; I
shall rehearse it to her."

I said nothing, got more in the shadow; but
remembering that he had never seen me except in miner's costume, and not likely to recognize me in my cloth suit, I ceased to fear
his eyes much, but was careful that he should
not hear my voice. I saw him where, among
many, he disposed himself to sleep on the
thick wheat-straw near the stand, and, as the
lights were extinguished, had no fear of his
recognition as I spread my blanket in a few

feet of him among the sleepers. I imitated
the others who had made pillows of their boots
and coats, lay on one blanket and covered with
another; and was determined to be known to
him in the morning. Presently he said, ad-
dressing no one in particular: "I have somewhere in the mines, if he's not dead, a friend
called Quien Sabe. Have any of you ever
met him?"

"No," replied several, "not by that name."

"Where did he mine, and what his appearance?" asked one.

"At such and such places," he answered;
"and he was a black-headed, dark-skinned,
rather weak-looking person—weak in the head,
I mean. I say '*mined;*' he never did mine
much himself. He always had partners that
did the work, while he played treasurer, ac-
countant, and the like. He used to be my
partner. I want to find him, now I have got
back again from the States."

"To go partnership again?" queried one.

"Well," he said, "no; but I want to be with
him awhile. He always needed a guardian bad
as a boy does. I heard he was killed by an avalanche. It is true, I fear; for if he *saw* it
coming, he was so absorbed in admiring its
noise and bounds he didn't have the sense to

get out of its way. I have written and inquired in every direction, and I'm now going to the northern mines to seek him; for
Leina told me to go, or she, or both of us,
would die of nervousness."

"Yes," said one, "you have asked me about
him four or five times since sundown. You
may as well be seeking a particular quail in a
chapparal full of 'em as to seek a man in the
mines and not know just where he is."

"I know it," said Tom, "'specially when he's
dead, as Quien certainly is. A miner told me
out at the store if I'd go to the d—l I should
find him sooner than to hunt him anywhere
else; that, no doubt, he was toasting now down
below, or words to that effect. And I shall
quit the hunt—he's dead, no doubt, if not
worse."

I was tired of it by this time, and sat up in
my shirt-sleeves in a position where his eyes
would rest upon me, and said, "Pike," and
struck a match. He leaped about three feet
straight up, how I can't understand, caught
half-bent on his feet, and with a hand on each
knee gazed into my face, and exclaimed: "*My
heavens, Quien! is it you? And not dead!*"

"Nor at the d—l, either," I said, "unless you
and he are the same. Who said I was dead?"

"Wyche," he answered.

"Is Wyche in New York?"

"No," he replied, "he's in Mexico; but he stopped at the ranch in Los Angeles several weeks ago on his way there."

"Tom," I queried, "you haven't settled in California after breathing out such gloomy adjectives against it as you did that day in the foot-hill mines?"

"Yes," he answered, "I have, and forever, in 'the Valley of the Angels,' and I have a model farm, and library, and some — goats. And you must go eat grapes and oranges with Leina and the children. They are dying to see you—told me not to come back without you, Quien. They have made me tell more stories about you than ever Robinson Crusoe invented; and I am seeking you more in self-defense than for friendship's sake."

And next day we were bounding southward on stage and wave. His farming was successful, for though the laborers listened to Tom's directions, I noticed they did contrary to them.

Albeit the ranch was a model one. For nature here had unrolled a valley like a rare variegated carpet, fitted around little hills, sprinkled it with flowers and rich grasses; and art had grouped a villa of cozy cottages upon a bright knoll in an orange and lemon grove whose green and yellow orbs, some smaller, some larger, were like bolls of beryl and gold among the green leaves and white blossoms; and flanked it here and there with figs and grapes in fruitful bowers and borders. The crisp sunshine, the breezes from the hidden sea, the voluptuous atmospheric sensations and aspects, imparted to every object a charm that is surely seen nowhere else. Within doors love's trustful peace dwelt. The children, the dogs, the cats, and birds were at home. The scattered herds and flocks, flecking the landscape, knew Tom's call, and ran to him on sight as assured of his friendship. And Leina, unconscious of the guide and guard she was to him, was cheerful and reposeful in his presence, like a glorious flower softly reveling in caressing sunshine, tinting its cheeks, touching their graces with freshness and fragrance evermore.

www.ingramcontent.com/pod-product-compliance
Lightning Source LLC
Chambersburg PA
CBHW060606030726
47498CB00005B/1566